"The Chateau And The Vineyard?" Remy Asked.

"I'm willing to part with them."

The wind howled. Amelia lifted her wine glass, and the pinot grigio slipped down her throat like cool silk.

"Then I see no reason why we can't wrap up this negotiation tonight," he said.

"I don't think so," she replied.

"My family wants this property," he said. "Very much. The price has always been negotiable. You say you'll sell. So what will it take to make you a happy seller?"

"You," she said, staring at the flagstones like a shy schoolgirl instead of a wanton seductress. "For a month."

Dear Reader,

When I began this book, I thought, wouldn't it be fun to inherit a vineyard in Provence and meet a handsome French *comte* who wants both the vineyard and me? Amelia, my heroine, comes from a family of women who are taught from birth to marry well. She's a rebel. The book begins with her breaking up with a longtime boyfriend who didn't value her. Of course, it's she who doesn't really value herself. When her favorite aunt dies and leaves her a vineyard, she goes to France. Who should show up to claim it but an incredibly sexy man who has ancient rights to it himself.

After a night with him, he made her feel so desirable she wants him to teach her about love. She makes him an offer—if you make me your mistress for a month, I'll sell you the vineyard.

This novel is about self-doubt and fantasy and adventure. It's about a woman who meets a man who's wealthy but who's lost his soul. Because of love and commitment both become much more than they ever imagined possible.

Enjoy.

Ann Major

ANN MAJOR

MISTRESS FOR A MONTH

Published by Silhouette Books
America's Publisher of Contemporary Romance

ISBN-13: 978-0-373-76869-1
ISBN-10: 0-373-76869-9

MISTRESS FOR A MONTH

This edition published by arrangement with Harlequin Books S.A.

Visit Silhouette Books at www.eHarlequin.com

Printed in U.S.A.

Recent Books by Ann Major

Silhouette Desire

Love Me True #1213
Midnight Fantasy #1304
Cowboy Fantasy #1375
A Cowboy & a Gentleman #1477
Shameless #1513
The Bride Tamer #1586
The Amalfi Bride #1784
Sold Into Marriage #1832
Mistress for a Month #1869

ANN MAJOR

lives in Texas with her husband of many years and is the mother of three grown children. She has a master's degree from Texas A&M at Kingsville, Texas, and is a former English teacher. She is a founding board member of the Romance Writers of America and a frequent speaker at writers' groups.

Ann loves to write; she considers her ability to do so a gift. Her hobbies include hiking in the mountains, sailing, ocean kayaking, traveling and playing the piano. But most of all she enjoys her family.

To my aunt, Patricia Carson Major, because she's
so much fun and she adores all things French.
Unfortunately, she never married a French *comte.*
At least, not yet.

One

North Shore
Oahu, Hawaii

Wild, zany Aunt Tate dead?

Amelia flipped her cell phone shut. Then her grip tightened on her steering wheel as she rounded a curve of green mountain, and the tall hotels of Waikiki vanished in her rearview mirror. Why couldn't her mother ever just answer the phone?

Amy punched in her mother's number once more, and again it rang and rang.

After Aunt Tate's horrid French attorney had told her her aunt had died, Amy had stopped listening for a second or two. The next thing she'd caught was, "She left you everything."

Everything should have included only Château Serene and the vineyard in Provence where Amy had once shared sparkling summers with Aunt Tate and her haughty *comte,* but her aunt had not quite finished the process of donating her extremely valuable Matisse to a French museum before her death. She'd left a letter to Amy in her will stating her intentions regarding the painting, but technically the Matisse was hers, as well.

"I'm afraid the property is in a pitiable state of neglect. Luckily for you the young *comte* is ready to make you a generous offer. Naturally he would like to buy the painting back, as well. Surely it belongs on the wall in the home of the family who's owned it for nearly a century."

"The *comte*'s family disliked my aunt. I'm not sure I want to sell to him!"

"But, mademoiselle, the château belonged to his family for nearly eight hundred years."

"Well, *apparently* everything belongs to me now. Goodbye!"

She'd immediately called Nan, her best friend, who'd been in a sulk because she hadn't gotten to go on a retreat on Molokai with her sister Liz and had asked her to cover for her at Vintage, her resale shop, during the sale today. Then she'd tried to call her mother to tell her about Tate and to ask her if she'd work at Vintage so that she could fly to France to check on the château and vineyard.

Imagining her customers lined up outside Vintage, Amy pressed the accelerator, speeding through the mountains and then along the rugged coastline where waves exploded against the rocks. The shop didn't matter. Nothing mattered. Life was short. She wanted Fletcher, her longtime boyfriend. She wanted his arms around her. That was why she was driving as fast as she could to his beach house on the North Shore.

Aunt Tate was gone. On a day like this there should be a rogue wave hurtling toward the Hawaiian Islands or an earthquake about to topple the hotels in Waikiki.

Despite the wind pounding the hood of her Toyota and streaming past her windows, the North Shore of Oahu with its lush, green mountains and wide, white beaches and ocean was beautiful.

Amy felt sad and restless and increasingly nostalgic about Aunt Tate as she kept redialing her mother. If only she could reach her.

I'll never watch Aunt Tate put on one of her crazy get-ups again. I'll never hear her throaty laugh as she bows extravagantly and jokes about being a countess.

The bright blue sky misted. Amy's eyes burned.

No! She wasn't crying!

She was driving too fast, and she never drove too fast. With a shaking hand she dialed her mother again, only this time she mashed her cell phone against her ear.

Sounding out of breath, her mother caught the phone on the eighth ring. "Hello!"

"Mom! *Finally!* The most awful thing has happened! I've been calling you and calling you. For hours." The last was an exaggeration, but her mother deserved it.

"Do you need more money? Me to sign another mortgage paper on Vintage? Where are you, sweetie? You're breaking up. Isn't today your big day? How's the sale going?"

"Mom, I'm not at Vintage. I'm on the North Shore."

"Amelia, I thought *we* agreed you weren't going to chase Fletcher any more!"

Do moms ever step out of the mom role? The last thing she needed was for her mom to start in on how irresponsible and indifferent Fletcher was. Why had she called her mom, of all people?

Because Carol, favorite daughter, *her* sister, had married well—an English lord, no less. Carol lived on an estate an hour out of London, and it was in the middle of the night over there. Because her best girl buddy, Liz, was in Molokai sitting cross-legged at a retreat. Because Fletcher's phone was turned off as usual. Because Mom *was* Tate's sister. Because she was her mom, for heaven's sake. And if she had to go to France, who would take care of Vintage?

Shells crunched under Amy's tires as she braked in front of Fletcher's unpainted house. As always the house and neighborhood looked so shabby they creeped her out.

"*Amelia!* Tell me you didn't drive out to Fletcher's alone!"

Amy gritted her teeth.

"You could do so much better."

"Mother, I'm grown."

"Sometimes I wonder. Carol wouldn't have wasted her precious time—"

"Don't start on Carol, either!"

"This is all your father's fault. He was a loser, but you were his favorite. And you couldn't see through him. You feel comfortable with losers like him."

"You married him."

"Don't remind me."

"Mother!"

"Not that I'm glad he left me or that's he's dead, God rest his soul."

From her car Amy nervously scanned the broken-down cars and trucks in Fletcher's front yard. Then she spotted

Fletcher's yellow longboard in the bed of his old blue pickup and felt a surge of relief.

Her mother sighed.

Amy had never liked the house he'd bought and rented out to surfers or the communal lifestyle that went with it, but real-estate prices were high on Oahu. She was hardly in a position to criticize. Here, people of ordinary means had to compromise. Since the value of her mother's house had appreciated exponentially over the past two decades, Amy had had to move there to save on rent and to help her mom with the property taxes.

"Amelia, are you still there?"

Amy's fingers traced the smooth leather of the steering wheel. "Mom, listen. This lawyer from France with a snotty accent and way too much attitude called me."

"What did he want?"

"Aunt Tate died in her sleep last week."

"I—I can't believe this. I—I just talked to Tate. She said she'd been to all those parties in Paris."

"Mom, they already had a memorial service. She's been cremated and put in a niche or something at Château de Fournier."

"What? And nobody called her only sister? They stuck her in Château de Fournier? She hated that place!"

"Apparently they just found Tate's address book today."

Her mother was silent, in shock, or more likely a sulk. Like a lot of sisters, she and Tate hadn't always been the best of pals. Tate had done what the women in their family were supposed to do. She'd married up, way, way up, landing a French count the third time around. And she'd never let her family forget it. She'd sent newsy Christmas cards every year to brag about parties at châteaux after her glamorous stepson's Formula One races, trips to Monaco and round-the-world cruises on friends' yachts. Her stepchildren were all celebrities in their own fields. But the main headline grabber had been Remy de Fournier, the handsome, womanizing Grand Prix driver. Not that Tate had boasted much about him lately. Apparently he'd retired from the circuit rather suddenly last year.

After one of Tate's bright cards or calls, her mother would sulk for days, blaming Amy's deceased father for never having amounted to anything.

"You're not going to believe this, Mom, but Aunt Tate left me everything. Château Serene, the vineyard, even the Matisse."

"What? That painting alone is worth a fortune."

"Aunt Tate intended to donate it to a museum."

"You can't afford to be so generous."

"Mother! Your baby's all grown-up. I'm afraid I need to go over there to settle Aunt Tate's affairs, pack her personal belongings and inspect the property. I hate to impose, but could you possibly watch Vintage?"

"I suppose. If it fails, who'll pay the mortgage? I'll need a day, maybe two. After that, I'd be glad to. To tell you the truth, I've been a little bored lately."

Which probably explained why her mother tried to run *her* life all the time.

"Mom, could you help Nan handle the sale today?" This question was met with silence. "Just for an hour or two? Please! Just to make sure Nan's not overwhelmed."

Her mother sighed.

Amy thanked her and hung up. Now all she needed was for Fletcher to hold her and make everything feel all right again.

* * *

When Amy opened her car door, the wind tore it from her grasp and whipped her long, brown hair back from her face. Her sandals sank deeply into the shell road, making each step so difficult she was almost happy to step into the high grass of Fletcher's yard. With less annoyance than usual, she picked her way through scratchy weeds, beer cans, fluttering fast-food wrappers and plastic sacks. Usually she hated the flotsam and jetsam of Fletcher's front lawn.

Lawn. If ever there was a euphemism.

Today she was too anxious to throw herself into his arms, inhale his salty male scent and cling to him forever, to obsess over her issues with his bachelor lifestyle.

He hadn't known Aunt Tate personally, but he'd scribbled Amy a postcard or two when she'd spent those months in France. One-liners, yes, but for Fletcher, that was a lot.

When Amy reached the rickety wooden stairs that climbed the fifteen feet to his deck, she noticed four triangular bits of red cloth flapping from the railing. She picked them up, fingering the damp strings and then the triangles of what appeared to be the tops of two miniscule bikinis. When she heard music, she frowned. Was Fletcher having a party without her?

A singer cried, "Yeah, yeah, yeah." Then the sound of a steel-string guitar accompanied by the heavy thudding of drums.

Her throat tightened, and she flung the bits of fabric savagely into the grass. Avoiding the front door, which stood ajar, Amy put her hands on her hips and marched around to the back of the house by way of the deck. Rounding a corner too fast, she almost stumbled over a bloated male body. His beer gut moved up and down, so he had to be alive. But his shaggy hair was filthy, and his sunburned arms sported several tattoos. She didn't recognize the spider tattoos, so maybe he wasn't one of Fletcher's regular roommates.

No sooner had she scooted around him when she saw six or seven more bodies sprawled on the deck, over the hoods of cars in the backyard and across the lawn furniture. A boom of deep male laughter accompanied by wild squeals in the Jacuzzi made her heart speed up.

Fletcher.

She turned slowly. Sunlight glinted in his tousled curls as he squirmed on the edge of the tub while balancing two topless blondes on his lap.

Amy dug her fingers into the railing so hard a splinter bit into her thumb.

When she cried his name, Fletcher bolted to his feet. He wasn't wearing a suit. To his credit his handsome face turned red. "Aw, baby, you should've called."

The girls toppled into the Jacuzzi with a splash. Squealing, they grabbed at Fletcher's bronzed legs.

Horrified, Amy began to back toward the front of his house.

"Baby!" Fletcher yanked a wet towel off the floor of the deck. Whipping it around his waist, he stomped toward her, leaving big, drippy footprints on the deck.

She ran, leaping over unconscious surfer bodies, plates of half-eaten pie and overturned beer bottles, her feet flying down the steps into the chaos of cars in his front yard. But he was faster. Springing down the stairs with the agility of an orangutan, he grabbed her arm.

"Baby, I know you think you've got a right to be mad, and you do, you do, but I can explain."

His voice was slurred, and he reeked of beer. A smear of lipstick marred one prominent cheekbone.

She jerked free and stomped past the cars to her Toyota.

"Look, I know I should have invited you to the party!" he yelled. "But you hate my parties. You refused to move in with me. You never want to do anything fun anymore. Ever since you got the store, you act as old and boring as those old clothes you buy and sell. And when it comes to sex, forget it! You never want to try anything new."

"Maybe because I'm tired after working all day."

"Which you throw at me constantly."

"Maybe because I want you to grow up."

"Maybe I'm as grown-up as I'll ever be. I have money. I bought this house. I run it. So what if I don't have a real job?"

She looked at him, at the plastic sacks fluttering like ghosts in the over-long grass, at his unpainted house and then down at the beautiful beach. "Is this all you'll ever want?"

"What's wrong with this? My old man worked himself into an early grave. Luckily he left me enough so I can get by. I wake up to paradise every day."

The blondes, wrapped in towels now, were standing on the deck watching Fletcher.

Would Fletcher's girlfriends get younger every year?

Amy fumbled in her purse for her keys. When had everything changed? Grabbing her keys, she punched a button and got her door unlocked. Then she climbed in and slammed it. As she started the engine, she rolled down her window. He ambled over and smiled at her.

Oh, God, his eyes were so startlingly blue, so warm and friendly and sexy even now, but dammit, her mother was right. She couldn't live with him.

But could she live without him?

"You know what, Fletcher? I'm tired of having to feel lucky to be dating the good-looking, popular guy that all the other girls want. I want to be wanted."

"Baby—"

"You're not the only one who needs to grow up." She hit the accelerator so hard her tires slung bits of shell against his bare shins.

"Sorry!" she whispered when he let out a yelp. And she was. She was sorry for so many things. Sorry she'd disappointed her mother. Sorry about her dad.... Sorry about all sorts of dreams that hadn't panned out.

A mile down the road, she began to shake so hard she didn't feel she could drive without endangering innocent strangers, so she pulled over.

She had always loved Fletcher. To her, he was still as gorgeous as he'd been in high school. But this wasn't high school.

She flipped her visor down and stared at herself in its mirror much too critically. Normally when she wasn't comparing herself to naked teenagers with Barbie Doll hair and pole-dancer bodies, she didn't feel *that* old.

Today she'd been too busy because of her sale to bother with her makeup and hair. The wind and humidity hadn't helped. Her brown hair hung in strings. Grief hadn't helped, either. Her hazel eyes were red, and her mascara was running.

Images from the past swept her. She'd gotten a crush on Fletcher in kindergarten. By the sixth grade, maybe because he'd failed a year, he'd been almost as tall and cute and golden as he was now. Back then he'd been reckless and daring and the most popular boy in school, while she, Nan and Liz had been bookworms. Only, one day he'd run up to them at recess and painted a mock tattoo of a heart on Amy's left arm. Then he'd kissed her cheek and stolen her book.

Amy had felt like Cinderella at the ball with her prince. Her cheek was still burning when he'd returned her book three hours later and kissed her again. He'd teased her like that for a few more years. Then they'd become serious in high school. Or, at least, *she* had. She'd told herself she could wait.

She was still waiting.

But not anymore!

London
Three days later

Promise me you won't sleep with her.

When a man is thirty-five and famous—make that infamous, especially with women—he is likely to resent such a command, especially from his mother. Even if she is a countess.

Without warning the slim young woman his mother wanted him to keep in his sights—for business reasons only—sprinted across the street.

Not wanting to alarm her, Remy waited a few seconds before loping after her.

He frowned. His mother had nothing to worry about. The wholesome Miss Weatherbee wasn't his type.

Brown hair, thickly braided. Hazel eyes. Not ugly. But not beautiful. Nondescript really, except for… His gaze drifted to her swaying hips again. Then he remembered all the sexy lingerie he'd watched her buy and wished she weren't forbidden because that made her infinitely more fascinating.

From birth, Remy de Fournier, or rather the *Comte* de

Fournier, had had a taste for the forbidden. His mother and his older, brilliant sisters only had to tell him not to do a thing and he'd do it. As an adult he'd liked his cars fast and his women even faster—until the accident a year ago at the Circuit de Nevers at Magny-Cours had turned his life into a nightmare. Ever since, except for brief trips to Paris, he'd been living in self-imposed exile in London.

Yesterday the highest courts in France had decided not to charge him with manslaughter. As soon as he could make the arrangements he would be going home, which was the reason his mother had given for calling him. She wanted to set up a celebratory lunch in Paris with him and his first serious girlfriend, Céline, whom he hadn't seen in years.

He should have felt relieved that he'd been exonerated, that his mother would even speak to him. Instead, last night he'd dreamed of the crash and of his steering wheel jamming. Again he'd felt that horrible rush of adrenaline as he'd fought the curve and the car and lost, hurtling into that wall at 160 mph before ricocheting into André's car and then into Pierre-Louis's.

With the memory of André's terrified black eyes burning a hole in his soul, Remy had dressed and bolted out of his flat at four in the morning to buy coffee, returning to work on the family's portfolio on his computer. Hours later he'd still been in a cold mood when his mother had called to discuss Céline and her lunch plans and to put him on to Mademoiselle Weatherbee, who was even now sashaying, her cute butt wiggling, glossy red shopping bags swinging against her thighs, toward her sister's flat on Duke Street in St. James.

Why was it that the longer he trailed that ample bottom, the more appealing it became?

Usually he chose leggy blond models or busty socialites and princesses, sophisticated women, who knew how to dress. Céline was his type. Mademoiselle Weatherbee with her wide, trusting doe eyes and thick brown braid was not. Deliver him from naive Americans with no sense of style.

Still, it was growing easier and easier to look at her. The worn faded blue stripes of her vintage cotton sundress made her look innocent even as it showed off her slim shoulders, narrow waist and, okay, hell, emphasized that pert and rather large ass of hers and its moves.

Nice moves. Very nice.

What would she feel like naked under him? Would she writhe? Or just lie there? Damn, if she were his, he'd make her writhe.

His bossy mother's predawn call had annoyed the hell out of him, even more than usual.

"I'm too excited to sleep," she said. "It's all over the Internet. You're a free man. And...Mademoiselle Weatherbee stayed at her sister's flat on Duke Street in St. James last night! And will stay there tonight, as well! Since you live so close, I thought maybe you could...check on her."

"I have back-to-back commitments before I can leave London."

"So far, she's refused all our offers to buy Château Serene, and she seems to want to follow her aunt's wishes about donating the Matisse."

"Isn't she on her way to France?"

"Tomorrow..."

"Well, then, negotiate when she gets there."

"She's in London to do a little shopping for her store. I thought maybe you could meet her and work a little of your magic. But don't take it too far. She probably doesn't follow Grand Prix headlines, and with any luck, she won't check the Internet and the London papers will ignore you."

"I met her once, you know."

"Years ago. If she doesn't recognize you, don't tell her who you are. No telling what Tate told her about us. Or you."

"This town's enormous. If I can't call her or knock on her door and introduce myself, how the hell can I meet her without scaring her away? What would be the point?"

"Improvise. I'm going to fax you a recent photograph of her and her sister's address."

"You want me to stalk her, hit on her and entice her into some pub?"

"But be careful. The last thing we need is more nasty headlines."

When she hung up, Remy crushed his paper coffee cup and pitched it into the trash. No sooner did it hit the can than he heard the fax in his bedroom. Amelia Weatherbee was not someone he'd ever wanted to see again.

Even her photograph brought painful memories. Holding it to the light, he noted the same youthful wistfulness shining in her eyes. Only now, there was a bit of a lost look in them, too, a sadness, a resignation.

He'd met her only that once. What was it—seventeen years ago? He'd been eighteen, she around thirteen. She'd eavesdropped on a private conversation, and he'd vowed to hate her forever for it even though she'd been kind. *Especially* because she'd been kind. Dammit! Who was she to pity him?

Funny how that same vulnerability in her eyes and sweet smile seemed enchanting and made him feel protective now.

He'd forced himself to dress and walk over to her flat, where he'd waited outside, reading the *Times*. When the varnished doors trimmed in polished brass had finally swung open and she'd stepped out into the sunshine, he'd shrunk behind his paper. Bravely armed against the gray sky with her yellow umbrella, she'd looked bright and fresh in her faded cotton dress and scuffed sandals.

He'd been trotting all over the city after Mademoiselle Weatherbee's yellow umbrella and cute butt ever since. He'd watched her shop at Camden Market and Covent Garden, then Harvey Nicks and last of all Harrods Food Hall. But had she eaten? Hell, no! So he hadn't eaten, either. Because of her, he was starving and grumpy as hell.

Americans. What sort of barbarian instinct made her skip lunch, a sacred institution to any man with even a drop of French blood?

During the lunch hour she'd gone into a nail shop, where she'd had a pedicure and had gotten tips put on her ragged nails. A decided improvement. Still, she'd skipped lunch.

At the Camden Market, he'd felt like a damn pervert when she'd fingered dozens of bright, silky bras and panties, holding them up to herself as she tried to decide. In the end, she'd surprised him by choosing his favorites—the skimpiest and sheerest of the batch.

Why couldn't she be the practical-schoolteacher sort who wore sensible cotton panties and bras?

When she'd paid the cashier, she'd suddenly looked up, straight into his eyes. He'd been visualizing her in the red, see-through thong, and her embarrassed glance had set off a frisson of heat inside him. Not good. Fortunately she'd scowled at him and had quickly thrown the tangle of lingerie into a sack and slapped her credit card on top of the mess. After that, he'd kept out of sight.

But she was nearly back to her flat. He had to do something and fast. He'd wasted way too much time already.

She was on Jermyn Street, a mere half block from her building, and he was running out of options when a cab rounded the corner.

Yelling for the taxi, he'd sprinted toward it, deliberately bumping Amelia so hard she stumbled. Her bags tumbled onto the sidewalk, spilling lacy bras and thongs.

All apologies, he dove for the woman, not the silky stuff. He caught her, his long limbs locking around hers at an impossibly intimate angle.

When body parts brushed, she fought a quivery smile and blushed. He felt a heady buzz of his own.

"I'm sorry," he said, letting go of her instantly.

Those soft hazel eyes with spiky black lashes stared straight into his, and she turned as red as she had when he'd caught her buying the transparent underwear. All of a sudden she seemed *almost* beautiful.

"You! I saw you before..."

A shock went through him.

Then she said, "At Camden."

He acted surprised. "Yes, how very strange. Do you live around here, too?"

"No. I'm visiting my sister. She has a flat just..." As if remembering he was a stranger, she stopped and knelt to pick up her bags and the bright bits of sheer lace and silk.

Quickly he knelt and gathered up bras and panties, too, tossing them into her bags but holding on to their handles.

Eyeing his hands on her underwear, she backed away from him a little.

He kept his distance. "If you'd like to have a drink, there's a pub across the street, or there's a tea shop around the corner."

A passerby, a man, gave Remy and the black bra dripping from his right hand a sharp look.

"I'm really awfully tired," she said.

"All right." He dropped the lacy underwear into the appropriate bag and then handed her her things.

Her face again burned an adorable shade of red when she looked up at him from beneath those inky lashes, which were as sexy as her butt.

"In that case, I guess it's goodbye," he said.

"You're French."

"Yes, and alone. Big city. I prefer Paris." Deliberately he allowed his accent to thicken.

"Of course. I love Paris, too. I've been there many times. With my..."

She looked wistful. Was she thinking of Tate? Her quick, sad smile struck a chord inside him. She'd probably loved Tate very much, he thought. His father damn sure had. He himself knew what it was to chase ghosts.

"Are you here on business?"

"Of a sort," he replied.

"I like your accent. It's elegant, but not snotty. You know, sometimes French people are so—"

"I like yours, too," he said before she could insult the French, who were his people, after all, which might cause him to defend them. "You're American?"

She nodded. "I'm on my way to France on rather a sad errand."

The light left her beautiful hazel eyes. "A favorite aunt died. I—I used to spend every summer at her château."

Her château? Like hell. Still, Tate must have been wonderful fun for a young niece, who had no reason to be jealous of her just because the *comte* had adored her instead of his own son. For all her faults, his outrageous, American stepmother had made his father happy. His own pretentious mother had not.

And he damn sure had not.

Remy's teeth clenched, but when Amelia continued to stare at him, a stillness descended on him. Her nondescript face with those spiky lashes and naive gaze wasn't beautiful. It wasn't. But it was growing on him.

Why couldn't he stop looking at her? Why did he feel so…so…

Aroused was the word he was trying to pluck from the ether.

Abruptly he looked away.

She sucked in a breath. "So, you're French and I'm going to France," she said lightly. "How's that for a coincidence?"

"Yes."

"We meet in the market. And now here again. Why?"

No way could he admit he'd stalked the hell out of her. "I can't imagine."

"Maybe it's fate."

Fate. Horrible concept. He could tell her a thing or two about fate. Fate had made him the despised bastard of the father he'd adored. Fate had hurled him into André at 160 miles an hour and then into Pierre-Louis.

She was still rattling on as Remy remembered the long months of Pierre-Louis's hospitalization after the amputation. But at least he'd…

"I mean London is so huge," she was saying. "What is the chance of that?" When her shining eyes locked with his again, she must have sensed his darkening mood. Spiky lashes batted. “Is something wrong?”

Her soft voice and sympathetic gaze caused a powerful current to pass through his body.

He shook his head.

“Good.” Amelia smiled at him beguilingly. “Then maybe…maybe…I mean, if your offer’s still open, I think I will have that cup of tea, after all, even if we did just meet.”

A cup of tea? As he stared into her hazel eyes he found himself imagining her naked on cream satin sheets. Why was that? She wasn’t his type. He felt off balance, and that wasn’t good.

He should run from this girl and leave the negotiating with her to his agent. He’d had the same cold feeling of premonition right before the crash.

This is it, he’d thought when his steering had jammed and his tires had begun to skid on pavement that had been slicker than glass.

Every time he looked at Amelia pure adrenaline charged through him.

This is it. And there’s no way out, screamed that little voice inside his mind.

Run.

Two

If only she could look at him without feeling all nervous and out of breath, but she couldn't. So she fidgeted.

He was sleek and edgy and yet he seemed familiar, which was odd because he wasn't the sort of man a woman with youthful hormones onboard would easily forget.

Curious, intrigued, attracted, Amy couldn't help studying him when he wasn't looking. His thickly lashed eyes were brown and flecked with gold. The brows above them were heavy and intimidating. He had the most enormous shoulders and lots of jet-black hair that he wore long enough so that a lock constantly tumbled across his brow.

He was too amazingly gorgeous to believe, and far too male and huge to be sitting across from her in such a ladylike tea shop. But here he was.

Amy bit her lips just to make sure she wasn't dreaming.

Despite his powerful body, he looked so elegant in his long-sleeved, black silk shirt and beige silk slacks. So grown up and successful compared to Fletcher, who wore old bathing trunks and T-shirts.

"Have you ever been to Hawaii?" she asked, struggling to make the kind of small talk that beautiful, polished Carol would be so good at.

Lame. Did she only imagine that he looked bored?

"No. Why do you ask?" His deep, dark, richly accented voice made her shiver.

"Because I live there. Because lots of tourists come there and I thought…maybe I'd seen you. I mean, you seem so familiar."

"Do I?" Did she only imagine a new hardness in his voice?

He cocked his head and stared at her so intensely she couldn't quite catch her breath.

Continuing to gaze at her in that steady, assessing way, his big, tanned hand lifted his wafer-thin teacup to his sensual mouth. She was too conscious of his stern lips, of his chiseled cheekbones, of those amber sparks flashing in his eyes, of his long, tapered fingers caressing the side of the tiny cup.

A beat passed. His eyes scanned the other women in the tea shop before returning to her. She swallowed.

When he grinned, she blushed.

"I—I'm not usually this nervous," she whispered.

"You don't seem nervous." His low tone was smooth. Everything about him was smooth.

When she touched her teacup to lift it, it rattled, sloshing tea. "Oh, God! See? My hand is shaking."

"Did you skip lunch?"

"How did you…? Why, yes, yes I did! There were so

many things to look at in the markets. Sometimes I forget to eat when I shop."

"I skipped lunch, as well. Maybe we'll both feel better if we have a scone. They're very good here."

"Do you come here often?"

"Never. Until now. With you."

"Then how do you know they're good?"

"Reputation. I have a friend who comes here."

Amy imagined a woman as beautiful as Carol. His friend would be delicate—slim and golden and well-dressed, the type who wouldn't be caught dead shopping at the Camden Market. His type.

Ignorant of her thoughts and comparison, her companion was slathering clotted cream and jam on his scone. When he finished, he handed the dripping morsel to her. Then he made one for himself. When she gobbled hers much too greedily, he signaled the waitress and ordered chilled finger sandwiches and crisps.

Licking jam and cream off the tips of her fingers, she willed herself to calm down. He was right; she was shaking because she was starving, not because he was gorgeous and sexy and maybe dangerous.

She was perfectly safe. They were in a sedate tea shop with a table and a tablecloth, pink-and-gold china teacups and saucers between them. They were surrounded by lots of other customers, too. So, there was absolutely nothing to be nervous about.

"So, you haven't been to Hawaii," she mused aloud, staring at his hard, too-handsome face with that lock of black hair tumbling over his brow. "Are you famous?"

He started.

She bit into a second scone, and the rich concoction

seemed to melt on her tongue. "A movie star?" she pressed, sensing a strange, new tension in him as she licked at a sticky fingertip. "Is that why you look so familiar?"

"I'm an investor." He was watching her lick her finger with such excessive interest, she stopped.

"You don't look like an investor," she said.

"What did you have me pegged for?"

"You have a look, an edge. You certainly don't seem like the kind of man who goes to the office every day."

Did she only imagine that his mouth tightened? He lowered his eyes and dabbed jam on his second scone. "Sorry to disappoint you. I have a very dull office and a very dull secretary in Paris."

"So what do you invest in?"

"Lots of dull things—stocks, mutual funds, real estate. My family has interests all over Europe, in the States… Asia, too. Emerging markets, they call them. Believe me, I stay busy with my, er, dull career. I have to, or I'd go mad." His voice sounded bleak. "And what do you do?"

"I just have a little shop. I sell old clothes that I buy at estate sales and markets."

"And do you enjoy it?"

"Very much. But it would probably seem dull and boring to someone like you."

"The question is—is it dull and boring to you?"

"No! Of course, not! I love what I do. I live to find some darling item at a bargain price, so that I can sell it to a customer with a limited budget. Every woman longs to be beautiful, you know."

"Then I envy you." Again she heard a weariness in his voice. Only this time she sensed the deeper pain that lay beneath it.

"And you don't think I'm boring…because I sell old clothes?"

He laughed. "Don't be absurd."

"No, really, you must tell me." She leaned forward, holding her cup in two hands for fear of spilling. "Since we're strangers, we can speak freely. Was your first impression of me… Did you think I looked boring and old?"

He set his scone down. "Who the hell's been telling you a stupid thing like that?"

"My boyfriend." Why had she admitted that?

"Then dump him."

"I sort of did, but I've always loved him. Or, at least, I thought I did. Maybe he's just been in my life forever."

"So you're the loyal, committed type?"

"Well, anyway, I can't stop thinking about him. All day I thought about him. And the things he said."

His black brows shot together so alarmingly her hands, which still held her teacup, began to shake. "Stick with your decision."

"But I've loved him since I was five, I think," she whispered a bit defensively. "My mother disapproves of him, though."

"No wonder you cling to him."

"No, it's not like that." She smiled. "It's just that I'm not sure I did the right thing to break up with him. I did it so fast, I mean. That's not like me. I spent several years planning before I opened my store."

"Maybe the decision had been coming on for a while."

"But Fletcher—"

"Fletcher?" His handsome features hardened. "Well, you're not boring or old. So, you want to know my first thoughts about you. I thought you were lovely. Fresh.

Nice. Different. Too nice for me probably, but a woman I definitely would want to know better if I were a different sort of man—one capable of commitment. Sexy." He bit off that last rather grumpily. "Sexy in a nice way. You're the kind of woman a nice guy, who has a good job and wants to settle down, marries so he can have a houseful of kids to play soccer with on the weekends."

His dark eyes with those sparking flecks said much more, and she grew hot with embarrassment.

"That's sweet," she said.

When his hand reached across the table for hers, she jumped.

"Responsive, too. That's another first thought."

She yanked her hand free and tucked it beneath her pink napkin.

"This Fletcher doesn't deserve you. But let's talk of something more pleasant. I can tell we'll never agree on this subject, so why argue? Your love life is your choice. Not mine. I barely know you."

He seemed out of sorts suddenly, defensive, almost jealous. But that wasn't possible. A man like him, who was wealthy, refined and movie-star sexy couldn't be jealous of her. Especially not when they'd just met.

"I'm sorry if I upset you."

"So, you have a sister?" He was clearly determined to change the subject. "Here in London?

"Carol. Actually, she lives outside London. On a rather grand estate near Wolverton. She has a large house with a conservatory. And a lovely garden, too. That sounds so English, doesn't it? But she and her husband—he's a lord and a very important person, mind you—keep a flat here in St. James so they can stay in the city whenever they need to, which is usually four or five nights a week. She's a barrister, and he's high up in the government. They both work in the city."

"So how much time do you have with them? What sights are you going to see while you're here?"

"I'm flying to Marseilles tomorrow afternoon. But I hope to ride the Eye and walk across the Millennium Bridge. I'm sure those seem like dull and boring things to you."

"Quit running yourself down. We'll do it, then," he said.

"We'll?"

"If you'll accept my invitation. Are you free for dinner and dancing tonight?"

"But we just met. I bet I'm not the sort of girl you usually ask out."

"What the hell are you talking about now?"

"Just what I said. I'm not the sort of girl you usually hang out with."

"No, you're not. But maybe that's why I like you so much. Why I find you so not boring and old, as you put it, that I want to clear my schedule, which is jam-packed I assure you, and spend as much time as I can with you before you leave."

She was thrilled and yet startled, too. She was in a foreign city, and she didn't know anything about him. Except that he was sexy, and she wasn't sure that was exactly the best recommendation.

"I'll have to check with my sister. She went to Edinburgh on business, but she's going to try to get back tonight in time to have me come for dinner. I came over here in such a rush, and she had a calendar full of engagements and business commitments."

"I understand." He pulled out a little black notebook and tore out a page. Then he scribbled two numbers. "This one's my mobile. The other rings at the flat. Call me if you're free." Then he shrugged in that wonderful Gallic way he had as he handed it to her.

His deep voice was as heated as his gaze, causing her to shiver even before he placed the note in her hand. Instantly she curled her fingers around the scrap of paper. When his fingers lingered warmly over hers for long seconds, her own hand froze.

Soon the heat of his long fingers wrapping hers proved too unnerving. She couldn't think or talk or breathe. Not with her pulse knocking a hundred beats a minute.

"Why do you seem so familiar?" she blurted, pulling her hand away so she could put his note in her purse. She gasped for a breath. "I—I just know I've seen you before."

"I don't think so."

With a scowl, he picked up the bill. Then before she knew what he was about, he lifted her hand and brought it to his lips, turning it over slowly. His mouth against her palm and wrist sent her pulse leaping even faster than before. Then heat swept her body.

"I don't need to call you later. I'll go with you…dancing…everything…tonight," she said in a rush.

"What about Carol?"

"Carol?" Her mind was blank.

"Your sister." He smiled much too knowingly.

"Right." She gasped. "Right. Of course. Carol. I've got to wait until Carol calls. I forgot all about her."

He laughed. "You're wonderful in your own special way. I envy that nice guy with the job who's going to get you. Lucky man."

When he got up, he helped her out of her chair. After he paid the bill, he escorted her out of the shop and said he hoped he'd see her soon. On the sidewalk he lifted her hand to his mouth and said goodbye before walking rapidly toward Piccadilly.

Amelia looked at the little scrap of paper with his phone numbers on it. He hadn't written his name down, nor had he introduced himself properly. He hadn't asked her for her name, either.

Why?

He had impeccable manners.

Was he famous?

Why did he seem so familiar?

France's Highest Court Upholds Dismissal of Manslaughter Charges against Comte Remy de Fournier!

Her mouth agape, riveted by the news headlines, lurid photographs and articles in the newspaper she was holding, Amelia sat perfectly still on Carol's "bloody-expensive" sofa.

Remy de Fournier. No wonder he'd seemed so edgy. No wonder he hadn't told her who he was.

He'd killed his best friend, André Laffite, because he'd driven on bad tires on a wet day to win. Since the wreck, he'd slept with every beautiful woman with a title on the continent, heartlessly jilting them, not caring if he broke their hearts as long as they pleasured him.

So, they hadn't met quite by accident.

She took a deep breath against the hurt that threatened to overwhelm her. He wasn't attracted to *her*. He'd been feeling her out, figuring out a strategy to get the valuable properties he coveted.

Beneath the blaring headline were pictures of the crash that had ended the life of his best friend. Apparently Remy had been determined to win at any cost. More photographs of the wreck were splashed across a back page. There were numerous shots of Remy and the beautiful women he'd dated and jilted. One of the women had even made a suicide attempt after her affair with him. Not that the woman herself blamed Remy. No, she said he'd helped her through a difficult time. There was an awful picture of him smashing his fist into a reporter's jaw.

When she finished reading the articles and looking at the pictures, Amy felt sick. She reexamined them, anyway. When she was done, she shot to her feet and began to pace with the newspaper clutched to her heart. If half the accusations were true, she should despise him. Wadding the paper up, she threw the pages at the wall and then flung herself back down on Carol's sofa.

Bastard. Liar. Jerk.

A memory came back to her. Remy had been eighteen, and she'd been in the garden when the *comte* had hurled brutal, damning insults at him. Never would she forget the torment in Remy's eyes when he'd stormed out of the château and straight into her.

"What the hell were you doing?" he'd thundered. "Spying?"

"But I wasn't."

"Damn little eavesdropper! Get out of my way!"

"No. I—I wasn't. I swear."

"Liar."

"No. I—I'm sorry about what he said. Maybe he didn't mean it."

"Spare me your fake kindness. He meant it, all right. I hope I never have the bad fortune to meet you or your aunt again." He slammed past her and out the gate and she hadn't seen him for seventeen years. Till today.

And now? Outwardly he was much changed from the tall, awkward, angry boy who'd been so rude to her.

Fool. He'd been deliberately charming because he wanted the vineyard and the painting.

Still, he'd gone out of his way to make her like him. Even now when she should be furious because he'd deceived her so he could use her or so his agents could trick her, she wanted to give him the benefit of the doubt.

He is loathsome. So much worse than Fletcher.

But that woman who'd tried to kill herself had defended him.

Why did the bad boys of the world always appeal to her? Why couldn't she fall for some nice, paunchy accountant going bald, someone like Carol's Steve, an upright, type-A achiever? Or even just the normal guy Remy had described: the nice guy with a job who wants to settle down and marry so he can have a houseful of kids to play soccer with on the weekend.

If a hard-partying surfer was the frying pan, Remy, the womanizing, ex–Formula One driver, who'd watched her buy transparent panties and had made her pulse race, was definitely the fire.

She was lying on the couch in a state of utter depression as she tried without success to conjure up a dull ideal mate when the phone rang.

"Hey!" Carol said too brightly, sounding like her overly self-confident self. "I'm at the house. If you took the train from Euston, you'd be here in an hour and I could have dinner ready. The kids and Steve are very keen about seeing you."

The very last person in London she felt like seeing was her perfect, superior, drop-dead gorgeous, big sister.

"I don't feel too well," she heard herself say.

"What's wrong?"

"Something I ate, probably. Or jet lag. I'll have to catch you on my way home."

"I'm so sorry you don't feel well. I worked so hard all day just so we could all be together tonight. Do you need a doctor? Should I come to London?"

Guilt swamped Amy. She felt like dirt. Here she was lying, and Carol sounded so concerned and caring. "I'm sure after a quiet night here, I'll be just fine."

"Well, then, if you're sure…I really am tired after the trip. Maybe I'll just pop by and check on you first thing in the morning on my way to the firm. Maybe bring you a croissant or something."

They talked a little while longer, making tentative plans to see each other in the morning before they hung up.

I can't believe I did that! I've let him ruin my visit with Carol! My mood! Everything!

She stared across the room at the wadded-up newspaper.

All those women, women as beautiful and poised and perfect as Carol. They must've liked him, too.

He'd said he liked her because she was different.

Quit thinking about him!

Usually, Amelia wasn't one for hard liquor, but this was an emergency. She went to the kitchen, telling herself she was after a bottle of sparkling water or a soda, but the bottle of scotch lived in the same cabinet with the sodas, and it spoke to her. She grabbed a glass and poured a shot over some chunklets of ice. Swirling the glass, she returned to the living room, where she settled herself on the couch once more. For a long time, she just sat there, glumly sipping Carol's scotch as she glared at the wadded-up newspaper and the half of Remy's face she could see.

Then she stood. Crossing the room, she picked up the newspaper again. This time a photograph she'd barely noticed caught her attention. His stony face bleached of arrogance and any conceit, Remy was walking through the pits carrying André's helmet under his arm. All she saw in his hard features was shock and grief.

Who was he really? He'd been so nice to her today. He'd been attentive to her needs, and he'd gone out of his way to make her feel special and beautiful. Was he that sensitive, caring person or the man she'd just read about?

He'd had lots and lots of women. He couldn't have had all those women if he wasn't a really good lover. He was French. Frenchmen had a worldwide reputation for being good lovers. She knew it was crazy, but she began to envy those glamorous women whose hearts he'd broken.

Fletcher had accused her of being old and boring. More than anything she wanted to be exciting.

Remy de Fournier had asked her to go dancing tonight. Maybe he was totally awful like the papers made him out to be.

Or maybe he was just the man she needed to show her how to be a more exciting and confident woman. He'd made her feel interesting and beautiful today.

Maybe it was time she learned a new set of life skills. What sort of things could he teach her if she spent an entire night with him?

Her mother was always saying she could be and have so much more if she refused to settle. Maybe it was time to live a little dangerously.

Slowly Amy dug into her pocket and felt for the scrap of paper with Remy's phone numbers on it. For a long moment she studied the flowing black letters. Then with shaking fingers she began dialing his mobile, but after letting it ring once, she hung up, and would have chewed her nails except she couldn't because she had on those new tips.

Damn!

She was still staring at her fake pink fingernails in utter frustration when the phone rang.

Expecting Carol, she picked it up.

"Did someone from this number call me?" Remy's deep, dark voice spoke with such tender concern she almost forgot he was the terrible person she'd read about and not the sweet man she'd met by chance and had liked so much this afternoon.

He sounded *so* nice.

"Me!" she squeaked, forgetting the terrible bit. "That would be me! The girl you bumped—"

He laughed as if he were thrilled, too. "I know who you are." Somehow the way he said that made her feel very special, like she was the only woman in the world who mattered to him. Which was ridiculous. He was a womanizer.

"I was afraid you wouldn't call," he said, again sounding so sincerely worried and humble she could almost feel her heart shatter. He was *that* good.

Or *that* bad.

Either way, this could be a win-win.

Hang up on him.

She plunged in recklessly. "I—I'm free tonight. Carol..." Amy glanced across the room at a silver-framed photograph of her blond sister and Steve and silently crossed herself. "We...we won't be getting together, after all. She...has a headache."

"Nothing too serious, I hope."

"No."

"Excellent. I can be there as soon as you can be ready."

"But I don't have anything to wear."

"I don't really object to that," he teased. "I could bring dinner over, and we could stay in. You could wear... nothing. I wouldn't mind. I swear."

She laughed. "You *are* terrible."

"So I've been told." He laughed. "What do you want, *chérie?*"

If she wanted lessons in love from an expert, she should say, "*You.*" She should say, "Yes! Yes!"

"Fortnam and Masons is only two blocks away. If I could just pop over there..."

"I particularly liked your dress this afternoon."

"I'll call you when I'm ready."

"I can't wait to see you," he said in a dark, eager tone that sent a chill through her.

"Me, too," she responded in a voice that was probably too low for him to hear.

When he hung up, she licked her lips with the tip of her tongue and drew a slow, deep breath. Just talking to him made her feel sexy and daring.

She exhaled a long, shaky breath. And then another. Oh, my God. She was so excited she'd held her breath almost the entire phone call.

Deep down she knew that if she were smart and practical, she would return to Honolulu and regroup. No way should she fly to France to negotiate with his agents or his family about the vineyard or even *think* about the Matisse until she had her head on straight. If she were smart and practical she would tell him she knew who he was and ask him to leave her alone.

But despite everything she'd read about him, or maybe because of it, she wanted to go out with Remy. Which was crazy.

He'd tricked her!

But he'd been charming, devastatingly charming. And he had not pressed his advantage, she told herself.

Not yet, anyway.

Her mind warred with itself, but soon the hunger for adventure with a dangerous, incredibly attractive man won out over good sense and logic.

He was a *comte*. Despite his many faults, that would cut a lot of ice chunklets with her shallow mother and brilliant sister. Definitely, he was a win-win.

Now all she had to do was to find a sexy red dress!

Three

Is nothing more tempting than the bad and the forbidden? Now that Amy knew who Remy was, he fairly oozed danger with every white smile and seductive touch.

Maybe that was why the evening with him was one of the most desperately wonderful evenings of her life. Not that she wasn't bothered by what she'd read about him or by her plan not to let on that she knew.

Her senses were heightened to an extreme state of agitation when she looked out her living-room window as she was putting up her hair in a clip and saw him at the end of the block, striding up Duke Street with a single white rose. When he rang the bell, her throat closed as if a fist circled it. She tore the clip out of her hair and ran to the door.

As he handed her the long-stemmed rose, did she only imagine that his expression was darker and more haunted than it had been earlier? Then their eyes touched, and he smiled. As she sniffed the delicate blossom, he stepped across the threshold.

"I needed this tonight," he murmured as he gazed at her. "You'll never know how much. You're like a breath of fresh air."

He wore the look of a hunted man, and she imagined he must have read the ugly publicity, too. Did he have a conscience, after all?

When she turned around, he gasped. "You look beautiful."

"I don't usually shop in expensive stores," she said, feeling pleased with the flirty red dress and silver strappy sandals that made his intense gaze linger until her skin heated.

Tonight he looked very masculine and elegant in black.

"You don't look like the same playful girl I watched buying silky, see-through knickers in the flea market this afternoon."

Blushing at the memory, she held up her new bag.

"Very nice," he said.

The ensemble had cost a fortune, but as she'd stared at herself in her bedroom mirror, she'd been thrilled with the beautiful girl she barely recognized. For the first time she'd thought she was almost as beautiful as Carol.

"Are those shoes comfortable?"

"Naturellement."

"But can you walk in them?"

She pranced back and forth in front of the sofas as she had in front of her mirror earlier just to prove she could.

"Wow!"

She picked up her hair clip and coiled her hair high on her head. When she secured it, he whispered, "Better down."

She removed the clip again, and he smiled as her hair fell about her shoulders again. "Much better."

She bit her lip and set the clip on a low table.

"What do you say we take a walk first?" he asked.

"First let me find a vase for the rose."

Later in the gloaming twilight when he took her hand and led her across the Millennium Bridge, she enjoyed the warmth of his long fingers entwined with hers and enjoyed the feeling that for the moment, no matter what their differences, she belonged with him.

A young couple was letting their preschool children dash about blowing bubbles. Remy's indulgent grins made her smile. Did he like children as much as she did?

The captain of a small motorboat looked up and waved gaily at the children and their parents. The children stopped blowing bubbles when gulls and a lone pelican swooped low over the gray, churning waters.

The little boy, who had blond curls in need of a trim, pointed. "Bird."

Remy smiled. "What a wonderful age. Life is so carefree. Do you want children?"

Nervousness tightened her throat, but she nodded, anyway, thinking it an odd question from a man like him. "First I have to find a suitable father for them."

"Not Fletcher?"

"Not Fletcher. What about you? Do you want children?"

His eyes darkened beneath his heavy brows. "I'm not sure I would make a very good father."

"Of course you could be a wonderful father—if you committed yourself to it."

"One would hope any man who fathered a child would

do as much. But I'm afraid there's more to it. One must have examples set early in life."

She heard gravity and doubt and profound pain in his voice as he watched the children race ahead of their parents to the other side of the river.

"And you did not?"

He had turned away, and he pretended not to hear.

When Remy took her to the London Eye, the immense Ferris wheel beside the Thames, he hired a private gondola and then treated her to golden champagne and a box of chocolate truffles.

She wondered if he brought the beautiful women whose hearts he'd broken to the London Eye, or if they preferred lavish hotel suites.

He asked her all about Hawaii and about her mother and her sister. At first she was reticent, but soon she found herself talking to him far too easily. Even the difficult years after her father had left and then died, those years when she'd felt like the ugly duckling in a home with her beautiful sister and ambitious mother, Amy described with affection and humor.

"I was too much like my father. He thought there was no point in being rich and famous. I missed him when he was gone. I think Fletcher reminded me a little of him. My mother was always saying neither of them ever wanted to grow up."

"A fatal failing," he said.

"Well, at least I can brag about my sister."

His eyes filled with empathy. "You are not the only one who has disappointed your family, you know."

Pain flashed in his eyes. "I could tell you a story or two. More than a story or two. Maybe someday I will." He pressed the back of her hand to his lips, and his voice was edged with such bleak bitterness she wondered if he was as disreputable as the man she'd read about. What was *his* side of the story?

As their capsule soared high and the city of London was spread beneath them, she stopped talking, hoping he would tell her something of himself. But he didn't. Instead, he pointed out the various parks, the Tower, the Palace of Westminster, Westminster Abbey and St. Paul's Cathedral, to name only a few sights.

"When I come back, I will see them all," she said.

He laughed. "I'd like to show them to you."

Would he really? Wasn't he with her solely because of Château Serene or maybe the painting? Was he between glamorous women and merely bored tonight? Or did he just fling lines like that to any woman he happened to be with?

"It's hard to imagine you sightseeing."

"The simplest things can be fun if you're with an enjoyable companion."

He told her he preferred St. James's Park to all the others because it had the best vistas and was the most royal.

"St. James's Park is the first place I'd take you if I ever had the chance. In summer I often sit beside the lake and work there. If I get bored or stuck on a problem, I watch the pelicans."

"In London?"

"You just saw one when we were on the bridge. The first flock was a gift from the Russian ambassador. These, however, are from Florida. They're quite vicious when you get to know them, sort of like our *paysans* in Provence who will squabble over anything." He smiled.

"And you enjoy that?"

"I understand it. When they fight over scraps, they take my mind off…" A shadow passed over his face, and again she sensed his pain. Did he blame himself for André's death? Was he really as ruthless as the papers made him out to be?

Her own conscience was pricked. Should she confess she knew who he was and suspected what he was up to? No. Even if he was not guilty of the worst, he had deliberately deceived her.

She didn't push him to confide. Finally he drew a deep breath and began speaking of London and Paris. His London that was made up of chauffeurs, private clubs and the best restaurants, shops and hotels was very different from hers. His London had nothing to do with vintage shops or flea markets. He never exhausted himself chasing about the city on the tube.

Not that he didn't listen and ask questions when she described her world—the shop, her bargain-hungry customers, her triumphs at finding something wonderful for them at some insanely cheap price, her life in Hawaii, which was both casual and laid-back, but ridiculously expensive and, therefore, stressful. He seemed particularly interested in hearing about her mother and her sister's sometimes unendurable ambition and conceit regarding Carol's grand marriage to her English lord.

"And do you call her Lady Carol now?"

"Just to tease her. But I must confess, I have a picture of Steve being knighted and a picture of her estate on a bulletin board at Vintage, so I do brag about her when my customers ask about the pictures. Actually, technically, she can't be called Lady Carol. Apparently, titles like that are acquired by birth. She's Lady Burlingsquire, though."

"Sounds very matronly and respectable. Old and boring, if you ask me."

She began to giggle, maybe because she was on her third glass of champagne.

"How about some coffee and a truffle?" he said.

Before she could protest, he'd removed their glasses and set them on a little table, which was too far for her to reach.

If he was bad, shouldn't he be trying to get her drunk so he could seduce her out of her transparent knickers and break her heart? To tell the truth, she felt vaguely disappointed that he was being so good.

"How's the truffle?" he asked, keeping to a safe topic.

She closed her eyes, smiled, sipped her coffee and nibbled on the treat.

"Delicious, I hope," he said. He pressed her hand to his lips when she wasn't looking.

His mouth against her skin produced so much sizzle she hissed in a breath.

"Quite delicious," she agreed.

"You must save the rest of the box for later," he said. "When I'm gone."

He threaded his fingers through hers, which were burning from his kiss, and pulled her trembling body tightly against his chest. More fire shot through her and she grew hopeful that he might be contemplating a swift seduction. Then she looked down and saw trees and the tiled roofs of buildings looming large. They'd run out of time.

As their glass capsule approached the ground, he fell silent, and it was an electric, shared silence that made her want to stay in this magical bubble, Cupid's Capsule, he'd called it, with her fingers burning and her body brushing tightly up against his forever.

She hungered for his gorgeous mouth. Hungered so fiercely her heart began to pound.

Why didn't he lean down and kiss her? And not on her fingertips! She wanted to arch her body recklessly into his, to mash her breasts against his torso, to taste him, to know him, to have his hard arms close around her with wild, savage need.

To be seduced.

She had to be crazy to want a man like him.

But the evil womanizer she'd read about in the paper did nothing the least bit wicked to further debauch his or her reputation, and she was so acutely disappointed she wanted to weep. All too soon, they landed, and he folded those tingling fingers of hers inside his and helped her out of the gondola in the thoroughly gentlemanly fashion that was beginning to frustrate her.

"Thank you, that was fun," she said, but an edge of strain had crept into her light tone.

"Yes," he murmured most agreeably, "it was." When he stared so intently into her eyes she feared he might read her thoughts, she looked down.

"Is everything all right?" he whispered. "Did I say something wrong? Step on your toe or something?"

So, he sensed her edginess. "Everything's too perfect," she replied, her voice clipped.

This time he ignored the edge. "I made reservations at a French restaurant on the South Bank. It's a two-minute walk. But we could take a cab if you're tired…or if those pretty shoes hurt."

"No." She found that she wanted to prolong every experience with him, even walking along a public thoroughfare.

The restaurant was styled as a 1930s brasserie. The earthy odor of truffles mingled with rich sauces, fresh baguettes and buttery croissants. The wait staff seemed to recognize Remy, or maybe they fussed over all their wealthy customers. Remy spoke to the head waiter in rapid French, and they were led to a table in a secluded corner. When their black-coated server brought the menu with a flourish, it was in French, which she thought she knew fairly well, but as is often the case with French menus, there were many long words and dishes that confused her.

"I'm afraid you'll have to translate," she said in dismay. She'd so wanted to seem sophisticated.

He smiled over the dark fold of his menu. "Don't worry, French menus confuse even the French. The chef has rewritten this one since I was last here, and I am unsure about many things myself."

She felt herself relaxing.

"The waiter will love explaining everything. And if you let him guide you, you won't regret it. In France cooking is our highest art form. Our chefs are like gods, you see. Like your rock stars in America."

Charmed, she smiled. "I always eat on the go."

"Ah, you English and Americans. Fast food is one of the worst things about modern life. But I will forgive you that transgression because you did not know better before tonight. You are disadvantaged from birth, you know."

"What do you mean?"

"American and English babies are fed the blandest of foods. Mush—food we would feed the chickens."

"But of course."

"No. Not of course. From birth French babies eat what human beings with taste buds should eat, foods such as sole, tuna, liver, fruits, vegetables, Gruyère, *fromage blanc*."

She laughed even though she knew he wasn't totally joking.

"The palate must be educated, you see. No hamburgers and French fries when they go to school, either. They are served a three-course lunch. Voilà! The child learns to appreciate good food. Even our lower-end restaurants serve excellent food. Not so in your country. You must be wealthy to eat well."

"Surely there are some exceptions.

"They are rare."

After a two-hour meal, which was prolonged by Remy's and the waiter's inordinate care in the selection of every course including the wines, he took her dancing at the Savoy.

Being in his arms for the first time all evening at the landmark hotel made her blood tingle and her body heat. Not that he held her all that close. No. But his hand against her spine burned through the delicate silk of her dress and made her imagine how his touch might feel without the gossamer-thin fabric between them.

It was beginning to bother her that again he played the gentleman, deliberately keeping her at a polite distance. She wanted to snug herself against him, to feel his heat and wildness. His badness.

Every time he stared down into her eyes while their bodies moved together in perfect accord, she wondered what he was thinking. Not once did he mention Château La Serene or the vineyard, but she imagined the painting and the properties must be heavy on his mind even as they danced what was left of the night away.

She closed her eyes and pretended that they were on a real date and that she was glamorous and fascinating enough to intrigue him.

It was two in the morning when he brought her back to Carol's flat. And he at least *pretended* he did so with as much reluctance as she felt. But after holding her hand for a brief moment and pressing it against his cheek like a lover might, he pushed the door of her building open and said an abrupt good-night.

"I—I had a wonderful time," she whispered.

"So did I. I wish you a safe journey." His voice was cool and casual, if a little hard.

Suddenly she felt awkward and shy. "I—I wish you a happy life."

"Good night." He let go of the door.

As the glass door fell shut behind him, he turned and began walking away, his strides long and graceful. Not once had he mentioned the château or vineyard or painting. Why had he gone out with her, then? She stared at his retreating broad shoulders with acute dismay.

Suddenly nothing mattered except that he was leaving. Hardly thinking, she flung the door open. Giving a little cry, she flew out into the night after him.

"Would you like to…er…come up? For a drink maybe?"

He whirled. Looking miserable, he shook his head.

"Oh, please…do come up."

As he stared down at her, his eyes were dark and tortured.

She knew exactly how a Frenchman, especially a man like him, would take such an invitation from a woman at so early an hour in the morning. Still, she stared up at him, her gaze probably too adoring and trancelike, and he stared back as if equally compelled by some dark force.

He must be used to women throwing themselves at him. It had probably happened again and again, especially in the glory days after his races when he'd been a famous champion.

Moving closer, he started to reach for her. Then he scowled and backed away, furiously fisting his hands. Shaking his black head again with more violence than before, she felt as stricken as if he'd slapped her.

Because she felt so vulnerable, his narrowed gaze seemed harsh and unrelenting. "I don't think that would be wise," he said. "You have that plane to catch, remember. Like you said this afternoon, you and I are very different sorts."

When he turned on his heel, she ran after him and seized his hand, pulling him toward her building shamelessly. "I want you to stay. So…much."

"You little fool!" he muttered, gripping her fingers hotly as he reeled to face her again. Anger and some other fierce emotion hardened his features. "Don't you understand anything? I am not the kind of man a girl like you invites home."

"That might be true under normal circumstances."

"I'm not what you think! I don't want you to regret tonight. That's why I can't stay."

She wasn't about to admit she knew who and what he was and that she didn't care.

"I won't regret it. I swear." She flung herself against his chest and was slightly reassured when she felt both his erection and then his heart, which was beating even faster than hers. She ran her hand over his abdomen and then his chest, causing him to shudder.

"You don't know what you're doing," he whispered raggedly.

"I know what I want, and I think maybe you want it, too." She touched his jaw and then his lips.

"I'm a man," he rasped, passion flicking through his words like a whip as he pressed his cheek and mouth against the back of her fingers. "But I don't want to use you…or hurt you like…." He stopped.

This from a man who wanted only a vineyard and a painting?

Her heart beat madly in her throat. "You won't."

"I already have too many regrets," he muttered savagely. "I don't want you on my conscience, as well."

"Then I must make sure that neither of us regrets tonight."

When he glanced down the street as if thinking to escape, her hands flew around his neck and she pressed her trembling body to his. Even though they were fully clothed, she felt his hard muscles and erection against her pelvis.

"In the morning, you can go. I won't try to stop you. I won't be a problem."

He tipped her chin back with a finger and smiled down at her gently. "You're not the problem, *chérie*." Suddenly his arms circled her waist in a death grip. For a long moment he simply held her, and she reveled in the heat of his great, hard body wrapping hers. His heart was still pounding violently when his mouth slanted across hers, unleashing a storm of emotion and other hot, licking sensations inside her.

One kiss and she felt weak and needy and yet powerful, too. And beautiful. So beautiful. Was this how Carol *always* felt?

He kissed her again and again, and each kiss was

more heated than the last, at least until headlights at the end of the street splashed their shadows against the wall of her building.

Then on an undertone of dark laughter and in a low, slurred voice she hadn't heard him use before, he said, "We'd better go inside before I embarrass the hell out of myself and you, as well, by taking you right here against that brick wall."

He tugged her toward her building. Not that she resisted. She smiled when the door closed behind them, locking them inside the glass lobby.

When she punched the button for the lift, he grabbed her again and pushed her against a black marble wall that felt cold to the touch. Here he devoured her lips hungrily until soon they were both shaking so hard she couldn't catch her breath. His hands sifted through her hair and then skimmed over her throat, her nipples, her waist and lower, his wide hand splaying intimately against her pelvis.

She felt a rush of heat as his hand continued to explore her.

"Yes," she whispered. "Yes."

Everywhere his fingers lingered, her skin burned in thrilling awareness. If he'd tried to strip her then and there, she would have let him. When the lift pinged and he pulled free, she ached all over with needs she'd never known she had.

"I haven't ever felt quite like this," she whispered. Leaning forward, she sucked on his lower lip an instant longer.

"Neither the hell have I," he muttered, his tone almost angry. "Dammit. This is the last thing I ever wanted to have happen."

Four

Inside Carol's flat, Remy bolted the door and drew her into his arms again.

"Nice," he drawled as his gaze lazily took in Carol's custom-made coffee table with the family photos in their silver frames and then the sofas covered in beige cotton velvet. Last of all he looked at her. "I didn't really notice how nice it was before. All I saw was you."

He leaned down and picked up the picture of Carol and Steve. Still holding her with one arm, he said, "Is this your sister?"

Amy nodded.

"She's very beautiful. Like a movie star."

Like the women he usually dated.

"You're even lovelier, though."

He was staring at her with the laser focus of a man deeply attracted to a woman. The shadowy room was as quiet as a tomb, and it felt a whole lot smaller with him filling it.

Did he mean what he'd said, or was that just the sort of thing he said to every woman? Seconds ticked by.

Suddenly the tension was too much for her. Feeling embarrassed and out of her depth, she loosened herself from his grip and rushed to the window overlooking the street and opened it.

The night air held a slight chill, and she shivered. Somewhere a siren screamed.

Staring out at the glistening pavement and breathing in the damp, she didn't dare look at him again for fear she'd reconsider what she was about to do.

"I've never done this, you know," she said shyly, still feeling too unsure to face him. Funny, even as she said this, she felt as if the rest of her life had never existed, and as if all that would ever matter was being with him.

He moved behind her stealthily, and she gasped when his warm fingers lifted the black silk shawl from her shoulders and a cool breath of air stole across her naked skin.

"Done what?" he drawled against her ear in that deep voice, which made the last thread of her common sense unravel.

His warm breath against the back of her neck made her shake, or was it his hand moving over her that so affected her?

"Slept with a man the first day I met him."

"Who said we're going to sleep?"

"You know what I mean."

"I'm not the sort of man who has a right to care if you've slept with a dozen other men."

"You prefer an experienced woman?"

"Did I say that?" he whispered.

"You probably do this all the time."

For an instant that haunted look she hated came into his eyes. "Not lately. But, yes, in the past. I'm not proud of it. But I didn't want it to be like that with you."

"Why not?"

"I don't know. Maybe I don't want to be the person I've been most of my life. Or maybe I just think you deserve someone better than me."

She felt a flicker of conscience. What would he think of her if he discovered that his badness was the reason she'd invited him up? Would that ruin his good opinion of her?

"So, you think a person can change?" she said to divert him.

"You're not asking a man who knows much about such things."

"Then what do you know about?"

"Hell. Did you invite me up here just to talk?"

Before she could answer, his mouth touched the back of her neck and began to nibble with a practiced expertise that made exquisite little shudders ripple through her. Even as new longings flooded her, his callused finger feathered across the softness of her throat and moved lower to caress her breasts.

"Incredible," he said as her nipple peaked beneath a fingertip.

When he began untying the delicate silk straps that held her halter top up and more intense pleasurable sensations pulsed through her, she sucked in a breath.

She felt weak, blindsided by her own needs. Losing her nerve, she gave a little cry and grabbed the straps. Holding them up, she danced away from him and hit the light switch with the heel of her hand. Everything went black and she sank against the wall.

"I don't want to make love to you in the dark," he said huskily. "But I will, if that's what you want." He strode to a cabinet, punched some buttons, and almost instantly soft, seductive music filled the room.

"Why did you invite me up here?" he asked.

She was too aware of his tall, dangerous body, of his smoldering eyes searing her from the dark. She sensed the strength of his will and the formidable ruthlessness that had made him a champion race-car driver and a predator in the bedrooms of all those beautiful, glamorous women who'd hungered for his touch. Horribly, his badness excited her even as it frightened her.

When he said nothing more, the awful wildness began to rise in her again until she was so hot for him she wanted to tear off her clothes and turn on the light and spread her arms and legs wide open and lean back against the wall.

Why not surrender to that untamed part of her nature? Just this once? He of all men should understand and revel in such primal female wildness.

She began to undulate slowly to the music. At first her frozen limbs could barely move. Only gradually did her body come alive and heat to his male presence in the dark. Very slowly, she let the silk straps fall and drift down her breasts to her waist.

Too aware of him, she caught her breath and held it. Cool air caressed her breasts as she unzipped the back of her red dress.

Maybe he heard the rustle of silk or the purr of her zipper as it slid down or her silk gown slithering down her hips, because he hissed in a sharp breath. Or maybe he could see her in the dark.

When he didn't move, the charged, pulsating seconds ticked by slowly. Then he punched a button, and the next song was faster, wilder, its beat flooding through her like a jungle drum.

Leaning down, she loosened the silver straps of her high-heeled sandals. Kicking them toward him, she watched as they sparked like falling stars before landing softly right in front of him. With a fingertip she caught her transparent, red thong panties, which she'd bought because of a crazy dream she'd had about Fletcher, and stepped out of them. The darkness made her feel safe, but this wasn't about safety. It was about sex and sensuality and recklessness, about learning that she was a beautiful sexy woman who was not afraid of that part of herself, which until tonight she'd never fully explored.

She slammed her fist against the light switch, and the chandelier blazed to life. She threw her red thong at him. Then, bathed in light, she arched her golden body against the wall. She was wet and hot and trembling.

Dry-mouthed and mindless with fear, she froze.

His dark eyes devoured her.

"Voilà," he whispered. Her thong dangled from his tanned hand.

Her palms grew damp. "I—I can't do this." She stabbed wildly at the light switch again, but couldn't find it. "I thought I could."

He dropped the thong on the carpet and moved lightly, swiftly toward her. She was sobbing when he reached her. Instantly his hand hit the light switch and the room melted into darkness. Then he began stroking her hair and her damp cheeks, his voice crooning hushed words of comfort.

"Don't cry. *Chérie,* you are a magnificent woman. Very brave. You were made for all this...and more." His awed tone held her in thrall. "You are very beautiful. Perfect. Exquisite. Flawless. And I like very much that you're shy. Tonight I'm the luckiest man on earth."

Still terrified by what she'd done and the desires she'd revealed, she remained stiff and unyielding even when he began kissing her tenderly.

"There are many things to cry about, but not wanting to make love to a man who wants you as much as I do is not one of them." His mouth moved over her throat and breasts. "We can stop any time you want to. I'll go."

Amy's confusion and alarm seemed to dissolve under his gentle words and kisses.

"No! Don't go!"

"So beautiful," he murmured, kissing her damp eyelids and cheeks. "All night I fought this. Dancing without really touching you drove me crazy. I wanted you so much."

"You did?"

"I wanted you even in that damned tea shop."

Boldly she pushed herself away from the wall and pressed her length against his body. "Then I want you naked, too."

"Ah. Finally."

His strong arm encircled her. All too quickly, his kisses and his words made her feel so hot and desirable she forgot who and what he was and all the reasons sex with him was probably a really bad idea. Magically her tears vanished.

Wanting to touch him, she slid her hands inside his shirt. He felt sleek and solid and as warm as a baguette straight from the oven. She was desperate to have all of him. Soon her shaking hands were unbuttoning his shirt, loosening his belt and unfastening his slacks. In a frenzy she ripped his shirt loose and his belt out of the loops.

He was magnificent naked. Much larger, darker and more powerfully built than Fletcher. He had long, muscular legs and large feet, which she quite liked. She stared at his broad, square toes for a while because she was too shy to look at the rest of him. Finally her eyes traveled up his legs. He was huge and erect, and she was pleased with that part of him, too.

It was nice, this being naked together. Things were somehow simpler, more equal. No longer did he seem the *comte* and she the naive ugly duckling from America.

When he took her hands and made her touch him *there,* she took a deep, steadying breath. He began to stroke her, too, and she liked the things he did. She liked them so much that her hands began to move over his body with natural wonder and delight. Soon she was quivering from his slightest touch even as she felt his flesh respond beneath her lightest caress.

His low growls of pleasure made her ache for more, and her breathing quickened. He began to breathe fast and hard, too.

"Where's the bedroom?"

When she pointed, he lifted her into his arms and carried down the hall. Ripping off the bedcovers, he laid her down on Carol's fine, embroidered, laundry-scented sheets. When he straddled her, she ran her fingers over his wide shoulders, his furred, muscular chest and waist, her fingertips lingering over the warm, sinewy muscles of his arms and abdomen. He was stroking and kissing her, too, with an easy familiarity that made her feel she had always belonged to him and always would.

"I want you so much," she said, her tone low and urgent.

His hand drifted between her damp, open thighs. "I know."

"Then why don't—"

"You Americans are always in a hurry. Some things like food and sex are better if you take the time to savor them."

He pressed his mouth gently to her lips so she couldn't talk. Then he began caressing her again until her entire being felt radiantly aglow, until the slightest flick of his fingertip anywhere against her bare skin made her jump. She was now so hot for him that his lightest touch became the most exquisite torture, but, of course, it wasn't torture at all.

Without giving her any warning, he eased himself down her body and lodged his head between her thighs. Before she could cry out, his hot, open mouth began to caress secret silky places, his tongue dipping, circling, tasting until one flick made something burst inside her like liquid lightning. Exploding, her whole body pulsed. Screaming, writhing, she dug her hands into his powerful shoulders and hugged him closer.

Afterward he moved up and pulled her into his arms so that her head lay on his muscular chest. Then he patted her hair and stroked her cheeks as she shuddered and clung. Finally, when she was calm again, he brushed her hair out of her eyes and said, "*Chérie,* you are the sexiest woman I've ever known."

"I…I…I'm not really…I mean not usually—"

"I don't want to hear about other men."

He got up and left the room. When he returned he was

wearing a condom. He kissed her brow and lips before easing himself on top of her. Then as if it were the most natural thing in the world, he parted her legs, stared straight into her eyes so that she felt their souls were connected and plunged into her.

He stroked deeply, powerfully, his body and hers growing burning hot. Incredibly, desire rose in her again like an out-of-control fever, only this time she blazed even hotter. When he exploded inside her, she cried out. Then she began trembling and clinging to him as before. Only this time she wept, as well, tears cascading down her cheeks, which caused him to hold her closer.

Where was the ruthless heartbreaker she'd read about? The man who held her was as tender and compassionate as he was wild.

He was right. They didn't sleep much.

He made love to her again and again, teaching her exactly how to pleasure him. He was patient and gentle and yet strong, too.

She barely knew him as a person, and yet she learned his body that night. Never had she imagined that making love could be so glorious. And yet even in the midst of rapture, she felt a piercing sadness at the thought of parting, because she knew such feelings, however wonderful, would never have the opportunity to deepen into something more than this one magical night.

When she grew sleepy, he wrapped her tightly in his hard, warm arms, snuggling her bottom against his groin. As she lay curled against him, she tried not to think beyond the bliss of his body enveloping hers beneath the sheets.

She had this one shining moment. That was all she could ever have of him, all she must ever want.

He was bad. Not the sort for her in the long run.

But he'd proved to her beyond a shadow of a doubt that she could be sexy.

The next morning she awoke to city sounds, to the obnoxious roar of a garbage truck lifting cans and garbage spilling against metal sides, to cans crashing back down on the pavement, to the shrieking of sirens and horns two blocks away.

She sat up, rubbing her eyes and squinting in the brilliant golden light. Muscles and feminine tissues she'd never known she had felt raw and burned.

With a shy smile she turned to face the lover responsible for these changes in her body and nearly wept when she found no one there.

She hugged herself tightly, fighting tears. He'd left without even a goodbye.

Feeling bereft, she hugged herself. Had he been real? Only those tender, well-used tissues and the dent in the pillow where his head had been told her she hadn't dreamed him.

Chérie, *you are the sexiest woman I've ever known.*

She lay back, thoughtfully stroking the pillow that still carried his scent. Remembering how he'd sucked her naked breasts so lovingly, she threw off the covers so that the warm sunlight could stream across her and heat her skin as his mouth and tongue had. She ran her palm over her belly, and as she thought of his lips on her flesh, her stomach quivered and perspiration beaded her brow.

Oh, God! She was pathetic. She wanted him more than ever.

She sat up. With a feral scream, she threw his pillow at the wall and then shot out of bed. Thinking she would go mad if she didn't get out of the apartment, she raced toward the bathroom just as the phone rang.

Thinking it was Remy, she lunged for it. *Pathetic!* Maybe she should confess she'd known all along who he was. No! Then he'd *really* know she was pathetic.

"Hello there," she murmured.

"You don't sound at all well," Carol said, her tone anxious and much too big sisterly.

An acute shudder of disappointment moved through Amy, but she forced herself to get a grip. Putting her hand over the receiver, she closed her eyes and drew a long, steadying breath.

"Amy!"

"I—I'm just a little tired, that's all," she whispered.

"You're all better, then?"

"Much better, thank you," she murmured. Stretching heedlessly, she gave a twist to her spine and made all those soft tissues burn.

"Ouch!"

"Amy!?" Big sister's voice was shrill.

"Sorry. I'm fine. Really. I am. In some ways I've never been better."

"You sound…depressed."

"Aunt Tate, I—I suppose." She stopped, horrified at how easily she lied.

"She did adore you. I mean the *Matisse…*"

"I'm going to give it away."

"Only if you're an idiotic, idealistic little fool, which knowing you, you will be!"

"Carol!"

"Sorry! It's horrifying how much I sound like Mother sometimes."

As Carol talked, Amy barely listened.

She was thinking about Remy and aching on a soul-deep level to see him again.

Would he be at Château Serene when she got there?

Or would he play it smart and avoid the hell out of her—unless she thought of some way to lure him back to her bed.

Because she wanted him again.

Five

Paris, France

Remy said hello to Marie-Elise, his secretary. Then he directed her to hold his calls and to make no appointments until the next day. Before she could say much, he strode past her into his own starkly modern office and shut the door.

When he flipped on the lights, his gaze went to the only decoration in the room—a framed photograph that lay facedown on his chrome-and-glass bookshelf.

He forced himself to walk over to the shelf. Carefully he picked up the snapshot of himself and André Lafitte when they'd been boys. In the picture they were grinning from ear to ear as they stood in front of their racing karts. They'd been fourteen. André's doting father, Maurice, who despised Remy now, had been full of pride and joy in both boys when he'd taken the picture.

Remy's hands were shaking by the time he set the picture upright on its glass shelf. He stood there, staring at the tarnished frame and faded picture in silence for as long as he could bear. The picture had lain facedown for a year.

After a few minutes alone in his office, he began to feel so alienated and full of self-loathing he almost flew back out to Marie-Elise's office. Instead, he swallowed and turned toward the window.

Outside, the morning was gray and bleak, but no bleaker than the darkness of his own guilty heart.

Slowly he turned away from the window and sat down at his desk, which was piled high with envelopes, flyers, brochures and telephone messages. Determined to accomplish something his first morning back, he emptied the contents of the first envelope. It was a letter from his estate agent, complaining that Amelia was balking. Several telephone messages and faxes from the agent were attached to the envelope, one with yesterday's date. The agent called her obstinate and difficult.

Amelia was the last person Remy wanted to deal with. He should never have agreed to meet her. Or kept his identity a secret. Or bedded her. Hell.

No use in thinking about her now. But despite his efforts to put her out of his mind, he constantly imagined her on the bridge laughing about the bubbles or dancing in his arms or writhing underneath him, and an ache in his soul would rise up to torment him. Determined to banish her, he wadded up the agent's messages and threw them in the trash. Then he slashed into envelopes, tossing garbage onto the floor beside the can with a vengeance. When he couldn't stop thinking about her, he decided to return his phone calls. Not that that worked any better.

Somehow he passed the morning slogging through the piles on his desk and returning his calls. When it was almost noon, and his desk still had numerous piles, he regretted his promise to lunch with his mother, whose preferences dictated long, formal meals. The hour was nearly upon him, and he was getting up to go meet her when Marie-Elise slipped into his office and quickly shut the door. She was a thin, efficient girl with a pale complexion. She always wore dark, loosely fitting clothes, large glasses and shoes with thick rubber soles so that she could move about like a shadow and not attract attention, especially male attention. He suspected she was much prettier than she appeared.

Once she'd implied she'd been in a bad marriage. She hadn't gone into the particulars, and he hadn't asked.

"Maybe you should go out the back way, monsieur. A man is here to see you."

"I said no appointments."

"I told him, but he laughed and ordered me to give you this. *Ordered* me! He assured me that he needed no appointment." Blushing, she handed him a business card. "If I may say so, he's a very pleasant young gentleman, monsieur."

Marie-Elise had never complimented a man before, at least not to him.

With a lift of his eyebrows, Remy took the card. In the next instant he was smiling, too. Then he was laughing. "Didn't take him long to charm you."

She blushed—Marie-Elise, who never blushed or took the least notice of *any* man.

Remy stared at her for a long moment. "His wife left him a year ago. You could do worse."

Again her cheeks reddened becomingly, making him think she really could be pretty if she tried.

"Sorry," he said. Feeling like an idiot, he rushed from his office into hers.

"Remy!" A short, painfully slim man gripped the sides of his chair and pushed himself to his feet. Gripping his cane, he steadied himself. Then he grinned from ear to ear.

He was hospital pale, and he looked years older than thirty. Years older than last year.

Dammit, he was alive. And his blue eyes were sparkling, instead of glazed with pain. *He was alive. Standing. Walking slowly toward him.*

"Pierre-Louis!"

"It's good to be back in the real world."

They hugged fiercely for much longer than was necessary.

"It's so good to see you," Remy said in a voice choked with raw emotion.

"No appointments?" Pierre-Louis teased. "No exceptions, your fierce little secretary said."

"I'm late to meet my mother and an old friend for lunch, or I'd suggest we go out. But you're always welcome—here or at the château. But then, you know that."

He studied the dark circles under Pierre-Louis's eyes. Maybe they weren't quite as dark as they'd been three months ago when he'd last seen him at the rehab hospital. He was standing, walking apparently. Remy tried not to think about the amputated leg that the doctors had worked so hard to save.

"You look good," Remy whispered.

"Thanks to titanium we'll probably be jogging together in six months. Hey, but what about you? I wasn't the only one who hit a rough patch. I'm glad you're back. At last. Wonderful news in the papers last week!"

"The newspapers want me charged. Hell, did you see the editorial two days ago where the writer said men like me make him want to bring back the guillotine?"

"They'll forget. But more importantly, *you* should forget."

Remy stared out his window at the brick facade of the office building across the street, which blocked the sun and made him feel trapped in its long shadow. "Maybe I should have stayed in London."

"No. Don't look back. Just concentrate on the future. I've recently taken a job with Taylor's team."

"Driving?" Remy asked, hoping his alarm didn't show.

Pierre-Louis shook his head. "Administration. That's why I'm here. Taylor asked me to look you up. Have you given any thought to what you're going to do now that you have these obnoxious legalities behind you?"

"Work for my family."

"You became a driver because that wasn't enough for you. And not just a driver—the best damn driver there ever was."

"A lot has changed."

"But have *you* changed?"

"Too much." Remy paused. "So what do you want?"

"*You*. Taylor wants you on our team."

"I told you before that I retired a year ago. For good."

"We don't want you in a car. Taylor wants your brains, your administrative and organizational skills. He's not getting any younger, but he's got the ambitions of a young man. He says we need men with your kind of dedication, brilliance and energy at the highest level if we're going to keep Formula One a global television spectacular. As the technology improves, you can help us make the sport safer and better. You can save lives, Remy."

"Taylor's a bastard to send you. You're the one person I hate saying no to."

"Good. Then maybe soon I'll convince you to say yes. If ever there was a born mogul of the pit lane and paddock, it's you, Remy."

"Thanks," Remy said, but his voice was cold.

"But no thanks?"

"Formula One is a murderous sport. Like I told you before, I don't want to have a hand in killing anybody else."

"It wasn't your fault that the steering jammed."

"Look, I've rerun that race a thousand times in my head. I could have taken that curve more slowly. I should have. I was reckless, out of control."

"We were all pushing the edge that day. That's what drivers get paid to do."

"I can't go back. Not ever."

"Just think about it."

Remy shook his head.

"You know, you're the last man I'd ever peg for a quitter."

"Hey, thanks. I know what you're trying to do." Remy hesitated. "I've got to go now. But it was good to see you. I'll call you."

"You haven't heard the last of me. You were there for me during the worst time. I won't forget that. On a different subject—how long has your cute secretary worked for you?"

"Marie-Elise? Cute?"

"Is she married? Children?"

"Divorced. One little girl. And she doesn't date."

"Maybe the right man hasn't asked her."

"Marie-Elise is sensible and sensitive. She's been hurt—badly."

"Marie-Elise. Pretty name. Very pretty." His eyes were warm. His smile was as big as his heart.

They shook hands and embraced again, even more fervently than before. Remy felt good that Pierre-Louis looked so much like his old self.

Remy showed him out and then raced down the hall to the elevator that went down to the underground parking garage. When the doors opened in the basement, he loped to his red, vintage Alfa Romeo Spider.

He started the engine and backed out, but when he hit the remote door opener and the garage doors rose, reporters who were bunched just outside on the sidewalk started shouting at him.

A tall man held up a grainy photograph from a front page of a notorious Paris tabloid.

Amelia—laughing as Remy led her from the Savoy.

Bastards.

Even though the shot was grainy, and her face was partially turned away from the camera, Remy's stomach knotted.

"Who's your new girl?" A cameraman shoved his camera against the sports car's window. A flash burst in Remy's face. More flashes and sordid questions demanding to know the details of the relationship followed.

Seething, Remy tapped the accelerator and inched forward. What he really felt like doing was hitting the brakes, leaping out of the car and throttling the bastards. But he'd slammed a fist into one reporter's jaw last year, and they'd gotten all sorts of shots of that. Then they'd sued him and garnered more nasty headlines, all in an effort to exploit him to better their own bottom line.

He grabbed his wraparound sunglasses off the passenger seat and slammed them onto his face. Without waiting for a break in the traffic, he jammed his hand on the horn and tore into the traffic. Tires squealed. Brake lights flared as he shot ahead of them. Other drivers made lewd hand signals. He roared ahead of them, anyway.

As he sped off, a dozen motorcycles stuck to his tail while others swarmed like maddened bees on all sides of him.

He drove faster than the flow of traffic, and the paparazzi snapped pictures from their bikes the whole time. Long before he reached the grand old Hotel de Crillon on the Place de la Concorde, he was furious. Jumping out of his car, he flipped his keys and a thick wad of Euros into a doorman's palm.

"Take good care of my biker buddies," he muttered.

The doorman blew his whistle and reinforcements ran to help. Leaving the shouts behind him, Remy jogged briskly into the sanctuary of the Hotel de Crillon's marble lobby. Not that he paid much attention to the opulent eighteenth-century Louis XV architecture and décor, which included sparkling mirrors and chandeliers.

The paparazzi were tenacious. He hated that they'd gotten a picture of her. Even though it was blurry and she wasn't named and he didn't plan to see her again, she might still be at risk. The last thing he wanted was that sweet girl to be hounded by the paparazzi because of him.

His mother's cheeks were even brighter than the peachy marble walls of Les Ambassadeurs, which meant she was well into her second glass of Pinot grigio or maybe her third by the time he arrived at her table.

While six waiters watched them in deferential silence, Remy leaned down to kiss his mother's rosy cheek.

"Sorry I'm late," he said as he sat down opposite her. "A friend dropped by the office at the last moment."

She folded her menu. "Anybody I know?"

"Pierre-Louis."

Her lips thinned. "Ah, yes. But I thought you said you were through with all that."

Anything that had to do with Formula One had always been extremely distasteful to her. No wonder. Her lover, his biological father, had been killed racing Formula One. Their affair had destroyed her marriage. Remy had gone into Formula One as much to even the score with her as to get revenge on the *comte* for detesting him. After that dreadful afternoon when Remy had discovered that he was the bastard offspring of her illicit affair with Sando Montoya, the champion Grand Prix driver, Remy had hated her. But time and maturity had lessened those initial hot feelings. After all, she was his mother, and in her chilly way she adored him—if you could call her obsession with running his life adoration.

Well, those mistakes were in the past now, and like many people with regrets, they could do nothing but move on.

Her remarks on the subject of Pierre-Louis's health were cool and dutifully polite. She was clearly impatient to move forward with her own agenda.

"I've invited Céline as I promised," she said, her dark eyes sparkling.

He smiled, wishing he could postpone seeing Céline.

It was strange. Before Amelia, he'd been curious about Céline. Today he would have preferred to dine with his mother alone. For some reason he needed time to get past that night with Amelia in London. She'd left him shaken. And not because he'd probably made negotiating with her more difficult.

"How did it go in London…with *her?*" the *comtesse* asked.

An image of Amelia's soft body coiled in a tangle of sheets that smelled of sex in a bedroom filled with moon-beams and shadow slammed into his mind so vividly his heart jumped into his throat and beat madly.

He'd felt an overwhelming desire to sink back into that bed and bury his face in her perfumed hair and hold her warm body tightly. And never let her go. Instead, he'd run. Even now when he saw his actions as reckless and selfish, he still longed for her warmth and kindness. He knew that peace could only be an illusion for a man like him, but he'd felt something awfully like it when he'd lain in her arms.

"Meeting her was a mistake. Nothing was accom-plished." Deliberately he kept his tone flat and low to indicate he had zero interest in the subject. "I would prefer to forget about it."

"What happened?"

"I never found the right opening to bring up the vineyard. She didn't seem to want to talk about it. Since I didn't introduce myself, nothing happened."

Watching him closely, she lifted her wineglass to her lips. Instead of drinking, she swirled the wine so that it flashed like liquid gold.

"*Some*thing happened." Her laserlike gaze seared him.

He snapped his menu open and sank lower behind it.

"I wish you were right. So…have you had time to look at the menu? Have they told you the specials?" He signaled for one of the hovering waiters.

"We can't possibly order yet." His mother closed her menu when the waiter came. "We're waiting for a third party. Perhaps my son would like a glass of wine to calm his nerves."

Seething, Remy spent far more time than necessary in his selection of wine. When the waiter vanished, Remy launched into a new topic. "I've been on the phone all morning with the engineer overseeing the foundation repairs for our villa in Cannes. I need to go down there, so I won't be able to return to the château until Mademoiselle Weatherbee is gone."

His mother's eyebrows rose ever so slightly as she continued to study him in silence.

"This *is* serious," she said at last.

"What?"

"You. You're deliberately avoiding her." His mother leaned down and pulled the same French tabloid from her purse that the reporter had shoved in his face.

A single glance at Amelia's grainy profile made Remy stiffen.

"You slept with her."

Since he was not going to discuss that relationship with his mother, he gripped his menu and studied it, even though the words were a blur and he no longer gave a damn what he ate. Fortunately, before she could continue to pry, a tall, slim blonde dressed in a black suit and pearls caught his eye and that of every other man as she glided into the dining room.

"Céline!"

Smiling, he jumped up and hurried toward her.

She was thinner since her husband's death, and there was a new sadness in her blue eyes that made her seem both fierce and fragile. On the whole, though, she was much more hauntingly beautiful than she'd been as a girl when he'd dated her in Paris. He brushed his lips across her hand, which was warm and satin soft. She'd been a sweet young thing in Paris. He'd always remembered her fondly.

She smiled as if she were very glad to see him. Suddenly he was genuinely pleased his mother had invited her. At least now, with his mother distracted by her matchmaking project, he would be safe from more questions about Amelia.

His mother's eyes were triumphant when he pulled out Céline's chair. No doubt she saw in the lovely, tragic Céline everything she most desired in a daughter-in-law—beauty, breeding, brains, style and old money.

An image of Amelia with her childish braid and faded cotton sundress arose in his mind's eye. Could his mother be so pleased if such an unpretentious girl were his choice?

Lunch was long and pleasant. How could it be otherwise in Les Ambassadeurs with the musky perfume of white Italian truffles, butter, garlic and fresh herbs drifting in the air? And with two such charming companions ready to shower him with their undivided attention?

Still, at least for Remy, something was missing. Despite Céline's efforts at flirtation, he was constantly distracted by visions and memories of Amelia's sweet face and of her intimate caresses. Why couldn't he forget how hot and silky she'd felt when she'd been naked underneath his body? Or how sweet and responsive she'd been? Or how utterly trusting? She'd been gentle and kind and sexy as hell.

Suddenly he wanted to forget about Cannes and rush down to Château Serene. What was she doing down there all by herself? Did she miss her aunt terribly? He wanted to put his arms around her and console her. He wanted to hold her naked and make love to her again.

Had she thought about him at all? Did she miss him, at least a little? Or had some newspaper article or old photograph of him she'd found in one of her aunt's albums made her hate him? How stupid he'd been to seek her out in London.

"Remy, what are you thinking about?" Céline's sweet voice chided when she asked him a question and caught him staring past her.

Muttering a swift curse under his breath, he forced his attention back to the lovely Céline. "Sorry," he said.

"It must be difficult…coming home, facing everybody…even me." She laid an affectionate hand on top of his. "It's too soon, isn't it?"

He froze, unable to answer until she lifted her hand.

She continued to flirt under his mother's pleased, watchful gaze, and he played along.

Thus they made it through their long, elegant lunch.

Did the *comtesse* hate her or what? Or did she simply despise having to deal with someone she considered so much her inferior?

Amy held the phone against her ear with growing impatience as the *comtesse* told her how disappointed she was that they could not come to an agreement, *disappointed* being a euphemism for *very pissed off*.

If only Remy would call, instead of his mother or his

agent, who were always so unfriendly and snobby. But no, he, apparently, was avoiding Provence. And *her*.

Well, if she couldn't have Remy, she'd much prefer to enjoy her breakfast in the garden in peace.

"Bless you, Aunt Tate," Amy whispered to the ghost, who she believed was still very much in residence, "for having stood the *comte*'s first wife as a close neighbor for so long."

"My agent informs me that you are going to give the Matisse away and that you still refuse to sell us Château Serene," the *comtesse* was saying.

Did she know Remy had contacted her in London? She would probably have apoplexy if she knew the whole story.

Bees droned in the purple lavender. A fat tabby licked its fur on a terra-cotta wall beneath the deep shade of a cherry tree. A plump black dog lay in a lazy coil under the rosemary hedge with a plump paw over his eyes.

Amy hadn't had her coffee yet, and the heat was making her feel as lazy as the animals.

"My agent informs me that you refuse to sell Château Serene," the *comtesse* repeated.

Amy pushed the phone closer to her ear, but the *comtesse*'s tone was so strident she pitied Remy and was soon concentrating on the purple shadows and sparkling sunshine, instead. What would Matisse have captured from this scene?

"I'm having breakfast in the garden alone. Do you mind if I put you on the speaker phone?" Sipping her strong, steaming-hot espresso, Amy punched the appropriate button.

"Are you alone?" the voice barked from the center of the table.

Much better.

"Quite alone!"

"Why do you refuse to sell?"

Amy stared at the pool and chaise longues surrounding it. Not that she really saw them. No, instead, she imagined Remy's darkly chiseled face and glowing dark eyes as he'd held her in his arms after making love to her.

Last night she dreamed that he'd come here and seduced her on one of those chaise longues in the moonlight.

"I had forgotten how divine the early-morning light is here," she said. "It's a gold haze, really. And I love the smell of warm pine needles, wild thyme, baked earth and lavender."

Happily the château with its crumbling biscuit-colored walls, its rambling garden and vineyard were in much better shape than she'd been led to believe. From the terrace Amy had a view not only of the pool, but of the lavender fields that stretched to the woods on one side and to the vineyard and village and purple mountains on the other.

"I asked you a question." Clearly Amy's enthusiasm for the place did not delight the *comtesse*.

"Oh, yes." Amy bit off the tip of her fluffy brioche swirled with chocolate and suddenly found herself dreaming of lying in Remy's arms again. "Some things are hard to let go of."

"That is how we felt when my ex-husband gave the Matisse to your aunt on their wedding day and willed the château and vineyard to her upon his death." The *comtesse*'s soft tone bit like a viper's hiss.

"I cannot sell you the Matisse. It is priceless, and my aunt's last wishes were for it to be given to the French people. As for the château, I like the way it has been modernized since my last visit, especially the bathrooms. Have you seen the skylights and the deep stone tubs and the showers? Well, they're really quite lovely. Last night after Etienne gave me a tour, I took a long, hot bath staring up at the stars."

She did not say that she'd fallen asleep wondering where Remy was and if he would come, or that she'd dreamed they'd made love out here by the pool.

"I never realized before that Château Serene was set on an area of Roman ruins," Amy continued.

"Who told you that?"

"Etienne showed me."

"Are you saying you want more money?"

Amy's gaze drifted to Etienne's stooped figure in camouflage trousers and a beige sweater. He was working among the vines where plump, purple grapes exploded in dark bunches. "The vineyards seem to be under capable management, too."

"Only a fool would trust that foul-tempered old devil. The vineyards are certainly not as we would like them to be."

"You seem extremely anxious to buy them."

Keeping her gaze on Etienne, Amy brought her cup of espresso to her lips again.

"Name your price," the *comtesse* said coldly.

"I need more time."

"I don't understand. You live in Hawaii. You have a shop. You need money. What could a girl like you possibly want with a château in France or a vineyard?"

Amy frowned. Annoyed, she said, "Do you always snoop so deeply into everybody's affairs?"

"Why won't you do the intelligent thing, the logical thing, and sell?"

"Maybe you should ask your son!" She remembered Remy in her bed and then her empty bed the next morning and the desolation that gnawed at her ever since.

There was an audible gasp. "What?" For the first time the *comtesse* seemed to be at a loss for words.

"Oh, did he forget to tell you? We met in London, I thought by chance. Until I saw the newspapers and figured out who he was. I don't like being tricked or lied to. If you and he want to buy the vineyard as passionately as you say you do, then send him. If I decide to sell, I'll discuss my terms with him. *Only with him.* Until then, goodbye."

Maybe her voice had been calm, but she was shaking. It was a long time before she could relax enough to find delight in the stone walls and shutters that glowed in the warm, golden sunshine again.

Remy. Just thinking that he might come increased her trembling.

This was the exact spot where she'd first seen Remy after she'd overheard his father yell something on the order of "You want to know why I've always hated you? All right, I'll tell you! Because you're the bastard spawn of Sandro Montoya, that damn womanizing Grand Prix driver, whom God in his infinite mercy annihilated in Monaco six months before you were born! I should have divorced the *comtesse* then! If you want a father, dig up his corpse!"

Remy. Bastard. Bad boy Grand Prix driver. Heartbreaker. Womanizer. And the present *comte*. Not to mention her tender lover in London.

Who was he really?

Did he want Château Serene badly enough to come?

If so, would he agree to her terms?

Six

Twenty-four hours had passed without so much as a word from the *comtesse* or her agent. Or Remy.

Where was Remy?

The late-afternoon sun with its dry heat was so intense the dogs and cats shared the same pools of shade beneath trees shrill with the songs of cicadas. Even with the shutters closed, the main living room felt oppressively hot to Amy. As she knelt over an album entitled *My Life—It Was Fun While It Lasted* and flipped through a carefully edited group of pictures that depicted the highlights of Aunt Tate's glamorous life, perspiration beaded Amy's nose and brow and glued her blouse to her rib cage.

The house was oppressive in other ways. Was that because emotions lingered in houses after a person died? Or were her own memories of happier days all that haunted her?

With a sad smile Amy turned the last page of the album.

Every picture either flattered Aunt Tate, showed her decked out in some outrageous costume or standing beside a celebrity or the Matisse. Funny that her last husband, the *comte*, was the only husband she'd included in this pictorial record of her life.

Mountains of boxes, stuffed with all that was left of Aunt Tate, surrounded Amy. Some were taped shut and labeled; some gaped open. Amy felt guilty about having to tear up Aunt Tate's house and sort through her personal things. Every time she put something in a box, she glanced over her shoulder, praying that Aunt Tate's ghost wasn't watching.

Life was short. With a start Amy realized she was thirty, which was half Aunt Tate's age at her death. Aunt Tate had already divorced two husbands by the time she was thirty.

Amy stood and went to the shadowy wall where a sensational copy of Aunt Tate's colorful Matisse hung. She flipped on the light that illuminated it, and the vivid colors came to life. The painting was of a small reclining nude. The *comte* had told Tate he'd fallen in love with her at first sight because she reminded him of his favorite possession. Tate, who'd been sunbathing topless on a secluded beach near Nice, had begged to know what he'd been talking about. He'd promised to tell her someday, and on their wedding day he'd presented the Matisse to her, saying she was the painting come to life, and that he was the luckiest man in the world. To thank him Tate hadn't worn any clothes for a month.

Amy was reaching for a red, blown-glass bud vase that she'd bought Aunt Tate in Venice when a loud knock boomed at the thick front door. Next, Remy's compelling baritone echoed through the house. Her heart began to race. Without even bothering to wrap the bud vase, she flung it into a box. Then she ran barefoot through the dark house.

The front door stood slightly ajar—he'd arrogantly pushed it open. Not that he was anywhere to be seen.

"Hello?" When she peered out the door, a shrill burst from the cicadas greeted her.

Had she only imagined his voice? Hating that she looked such a mess, she ran her hands through her hair and smoothed her blouse as she tiptoed outside onto sunbaked stone.

"So, you refuse to sell—until you talk to me?"

She jumped.

"I would have thought you'd never want to see me again," he said.

"I'm not too smart—especially where men are concerned," she said dryly.

He laughed. He was leaning against the wall wearing aviator sunglasses with impenetrable reflective lenses. His tall, dark figure was drenched in brilliant, lemony light that caused his elongated shadow to slash across the warm flagstones.

With difficulty she squared her shoulders. He shifted his weight from one leg to the other as if he, too, felt on edge. Then he fell back into his slouch against the stone wall.

"If this isn't a good time, I'll go."

His low, guarded tone caused her heart to race all over again. Obviously he was eager to run.

"No...it's a great time."

She squinted against the warm glare. He wore stone-washed jeans and a long-sleeved, white shirt rolled to his elbows. He looked good, too good. Taking a breath, she wet her dry lips with her tongue.

He whipped off his glasses with a defiant smile. "I should have told you who I was in London."

His hard stranger's voice made her chest knot. She swallowed, hoping that the fist in her chest would ease. Maybe she should confess that she'd known who he was almost from the first. Instead, she stared at him in sullen silence.

"I won't blame you for hating me," he said.

"But I don't…" She shook her head. "Not that I think what you did was right."

"You're too generous," he continued. "I'm not the most admirable person."

Guilt gnawed at her.

"But I expect you know that by now. I did warn you that you'd regret—"

She held up a hand. "Don't overestimate my virtue. And please stop with the apologies. I don't know what I feel, okay? I read a few newspapers, a few unflattering stories about you."

"I was charged and found guilty of murder by the media."

"Your steering mechanism failed."

"I killed my best friend. I have former friends and even family members who won't speak to me. André's father was my father's mechanic. As a kid I loved hanging out with him in the garage. He taught me about cars, about girls, about everything because my own father never took the time." His brilliant eyes pierced her. "And you and I…know why. Maurice Lafitte despises me now."

"It was an accident," she said softly, feeling a strange need to soothe him. "The track was wet."

"I was stupid, reckless, arrogant. I pushed myself and

the car to the max. Beyond the max. I was out of control on and off the track."

"Who taught you to drive like that? André's father?"

Remy moved toward her. "And for what? Surely not to kill his son!"

"To win."

"Yes! I had to win! It was the most important thing in the world to me then, because I had to prove..." He stopped. "I had to prove to a man who wasn't even my father, a man who was dead, that I mattered."

As she had in the garden seventeen years ago, she felt the heaviness of his pain and fought the need to throw her arms around him. "It was your career. You were paid to win races."

"Tell that to André and his father!"

He came so close that she caught her breath. When he raised his hand, she thought he might touch her.

But he lowered it, instead, and swallowed tightly. "I'm sorry. I have no right to want anything from you. If you're smart, you'll forget you ever met me. I have nothing to offer you. Not even friendship. I regret how I treated you."

"So you want to be as harsh and condemning of yourself as the newspapers?"

"My old life is over now," he said bitterly. "Fame. Easy fortune. *Women.* Funny, some part of me thought those glory days would last forever. They never do, though. Now I have to find a new path. I've made a lot of mistakes in the past year."

"Anybody would have under that kind of pressure. You were hounded."

"I've hurt some people I could have avoided hurting, only I was too locked in my own misery to think of them.

I went to bed with women to distract myself, never thinking of them."

"You're thinking about them now."

"When it's too late." His dark eyes locked on hers. "Look, I don't expect your forgiveness for deceiving you in London when I can't begin to forgive myself for it. But I'm sorry. I didn't want to hurt you."

His heartfelt apology only made her feel more despicable for remaining silent about her own deception.

"So why did you seek me out in London?"

"You know why."

Her heart sank. "The vineyard? Château Serene? The Matisse?"

"My mother called and told me where you were."

Some part of her wished he'd said he found her so beautiful and irresistible he'd had to deceive her.

"Because she wants them back?"

"I think it's a point of honor. Tate took her husband and Château Serene. Now she wants what he gave her back."

"And you work for her?"

"For the family. Since last year. I've caused them immense pain. It's time I repaid them for their trouble. And I am, even if ironically, the present *comte*."

"Yet you've stayed out of the negotiations all this week. Why?"

"To spare you."

"Don't lie to me ever again!"

She turned quickly, so he wouldn't see how stricken to the core she suddenly felt. Why did he evoke such wild emotion so quickly? So easily?

Placing her hand against the warm stone wall, she splayed her fingers and fought not to succumb to tears or more foolish passion. "You were afraid you'd jeopardize the negotiations." She hissed in a hot breath. "You don't give a damn about me—or about sparing me."

"Chérie..."

She whirled on him, no longer caring if her eyes were red. "Don't call me that. Not in the same voice you used to seduce me."

"You invited me to come up, remember?"

"Don't remind me of my stupidity!"

He held up his hands and fell back a step. "All right. The last thing I want is to make things more difficult for you. But you did ask me here." He paused. "Look, I've said what I came to say, so I'd better go."

With a shrug he turned to leave.

"Wait! The painting, which is in a bank vault in Paris, is not for sale. Aunt Tate used to tell me that an important piece like that shouldn't be privately owned. Before she died she was negotiating with several museums. She left me a letter entrusting me to complete the transaction for her, and that's what I want to do."

His jaw tensed. "That's very generous of you, considering..."

"Considering what?"

"That you're not a wealthy woman."

"Money isn't the only thing that makes a person wealthy."

"And I thought you were intimidated by your sister." His gentle smile made her throat tighten.

"Not always. And if you still want to buy Château Serene, you'd better listen to my terms."

"You'll sell?" His eyes narrowed with new interest.

"I live in Hawaii. What could I possibly want with a vineyard in Provence?"

"How much?" he said.

"Come to dinner…a little later…and maybe for a swim. It's too hot and I'm too tired to discuss business matters now."

"You cook?" His tone softened. "Not hamburger, I hope."

"Eight o'clock sharp."

"You speak enough French to know there's no way to translate eight o'clock sharp in Provence."

"You speak enough English to understand the term. Eight o'clock sharp. Bring the contract. And your bathing suit."

"Do we really need bathing suits…in the dark?"

His gaze slid over her with more than enough male interest to make her skin grow warm and her neck to perspire under her limp collar.

Which was good. The bargain she had in mind would never have occurred to her if he wasn't sexier than hell and hotter than the Provençal sun.

The sky was thickening with dark, rolling clouds as Amy bathed and moisturized and perfumed herself in the most intimate places as she stood in the largest of Aunt Tate's modernized stone bathrooms. Carefully she selected a translucent white thong. Next she chose a gauzy white dress, pearls and white, high-heeled white sandals.

When she finished blow-drying her hair, she barely recognized the vibrant young brunette who smiled back at her from her mirror.

Gone was her casual vintage look that made her look too much like an unfashionable hippie. Before her stood a sophisticated woman who could appreciate the best things in life, including a very sensual Frenchman.

Still wearing the same stone-washed jeans, now with a black jacket, Remy arrived fifteen minutes after the hour.

"Eight o'clock sharp?" she teasingly reminded him as she took the chain off the door.

"I did try to warn you." His grin was sheepish as she stepped back to allow him to enter.

He handed her a bottle of Pinot grigio. "I intended to return to Château de Fournier, change and grab my bathing suit, but when I stopped in the village to buy the wine, of course, Faustin, the wine seller, invited me to share a *pastis*. And when one led to another, he started in on politics, as he always does, and I ran out of time. Every time I come home, Faustin and I must have this same frustrating conversation, which he, at least, enjoys so much."

"And you don't?"

"What is the point of arguing? You can't change someone's mind."

The damp air smelled of rain and lavender and pine and *him*. She smiled, savoring his scent as she had when he'd lain beside her in London. "I suppose you're right," she said.

"You look beautiful." He grinned as he stood inside the foyer. "I drove through some heavy rain on the way over," he said, attempting polite conversation. "But that's normal for August."

She stared past him at the black sky and swaying tops of the pines and cypresses, but said nothing. He pulled the contract out of his briefcase and handed it to her. Silently she thumbed through the pages and then tossed it on a low table near the door. "Later. How about a glass of wine?"

When he nodded, she carried the bottle of Pinot grigio into the kitchen, where she tried to open it. But her hands shook with such excitement that all she accomplished was drilling out bits of cork. Her ineptness made him laugh.

"Allow me." When he swept the corkscrew and wine bottle from her, his hands grazed hers. Then he deftly yanked the cork out. "It just takes practice. Obviously you need to drink a lot more wine." Quickly he poured two glasses.

"Feel like watching the storm?" she asked, not wanting to be confined inside with him. Without waiting for his answer, she picked up a platter of cheese and crackers and glided past the stacked boxes out onto the terrace under the eaves.

He was slow to catch up because he stopped to admire the copy of the Matisse. A burst of wind sent leaves flying across the terrace when he came out of the house.

"I can see you've been busy packing," he said.

She led him to a small green table near several potted tangerine trees and sat in one of the chairs.

"I've made some progress, but there's a lot more to do. I can't stay here forever. I talked to my mother today. Luckily she's okay with watching my store for the rest of the month."

He leaned closer. "You'll be here a whole month?"

"Hopefully no longer. So I'm anxious to come to an agreement that is mutually satisfying—to both of us—within that time frame."

"And the Matisse?"

"Like I told you. It belongs to the world."

"An idealist." His dark eyes glinted.

"I don't know anything about art or museums, so it might take me a while to figure out the right thing to do."

"Maybe I can help you."

Their gazes met, and immediately she felt as if he lit her being.

"And the château and vineyard?" he continued.

"I'm willing to part with them."

The wind howled, causing the *cigales* to stop chirping in the cedars. She lifted her wineglass, and the Pinot grigio slipped down her throat like cool silk.

"Then I see no reason we can't wrap up this negotiation tonight," he said.

"I don't think so," she replied.

"Look," he said. "We want this property. Very much. The price has always been negotiable. You say you'll sell. So what will it take to make you a happy seller?"

When he gave her a quick, uninterested glance as he sipped his wine, she lowered her eyes and hesitated for an awkward moment.

"*You,*" she said, staring at the flagstones like a shy schoolgirl, instead of a wanton seductress. "*For a month.*"

She looked up, hot-faced and terrified.

Equally startled, he raised his eyebrows and gazed at her so long the air between them grew charged. "Me? I don't understand."

Her mouth felt dry, and she ran her tongue over her lips. Taking another quick gulp of wine, she said, "Remember when I told you that my boyfriend accused me of being boring and old?"

"Fletcher," he growled.

She felt rather than saw his gaze on her wet mouth when he whispered, "Damn him."

"Let me finish, please…before I lose my nerve completely."

Draining his glass, he swiftly poured himself more wine. He was as flushed with high color as she probably was. He sat up taller and shrugged out of his black jacket even though the night air was cool and damp.

"I—I told you that my life is dull back in America, that I own a second-hand store and that my boyfriend says—"

"To hell with him. He's wrong. I should know."

She felt her skin grow even hotter. "Maybe not with you. Not that once. Which brings me to the point I'm trying to make…"

In an agony of embarrassment, she stared down at her sandal-clad feet, which were cocked in a childish, pigeon-toed angle. Quickly she straightened them.

He smiled. "Go on."

"I need more practice…with an expert. According to all those newspapers, you're a very experienced lover. So, I—I want you to teach me to be sexy."

"Don't you know that those damn papers make up lies and use sex just to sell more newspapers?"

"But what if London was a fluke? What if I'm a dud the next time?"

He took a deep breath. Leaning back, his bleak, dark eyes stripped her. Then he frowned. "You aren't listening!"

"I know you usually date all those beautiful, wealthy women—"

"You don't know a damn thing!" He sat up abruptly. Seizing her hands, he stared deeply into her eyes. "You are a dazzling woman. Would you stop selling yourself short? *Believe* in yourself!"

"If you'd do this one little thing for me, maybe I could."

"This one little thing, as you call it, would compound the mistake I made in London—which was to deceive and sleep with a sweet, innocent girl!"

"If you'll make me your mistress for a month, I'll sign your contract for the price your agents have offered and not a penny more."

Shaking, she pulled her trembling hands from his and brought a fingernail to her mouth, but since she was wearing tips, there was no way she could chew on it.

Gently he pulled her hand from her lips.

"Don't! I hate that habit," he said, kissing the offending fingertip before letting her hand go. Then he shot to his feet. "No! Hell no!"

She stood, too. "Because I'm not sexy enough? Because I'm too dull?"

"Dammit, don't put another man's words into my mouth!"

The valley was thick with swirling mist and the sky was nearly black, holding the promise of rain. She stomped through wild thyme and made her way toward the grove of wet pines behind the pool, anyway. The damp wind moaned, tearing through her hair. Not that she cared.

Embarrassment and hurt at his rejection made her bend at the waist and hug herself as if in unbearable physical pain.

"Amy…" His voice and footsteps were cautious as he approached through the crackly thyme.

"Amy!"

In the next instant she felt the heat of his hand against her spine. She tried to jump away, but very gently he pulled her back.

"London was wonderful for me, too. I was afraid I'd hurt you. That's why I came over this afternoon. I've thought about you all week. I didn't want to obsess. But I couldn't stop myself."

"Don't say things you don't mean."

"Okay. Let me repeat myself—the best thing for you is to stay as far away from me as possible. Name your price, sell the vineyard and go home!"

Her hands curled, fake tips digging into her palms. "I named my price—you for a month. You're the perfect person to teach me what I need to know. All my life my mother and sister and Aunt Tate saw themselves as beautiful adventuresses who deserved grand lives. My mother failed, and I opted out of their game because growing up with such a beautiful, elegant sister made me too insecure to try to compete. So I never became the woman I could be, the woman you showed me I *might* be—if I ever dared to let myself…dare. I want to be good at sex, the way I was with you."

"Good with other men, you mean?"

"Yes!"

His fingers wrapped around her upper arm. "You little fool! Sex isn't a skill like playing the piano. When a woman gives herself to a man, she gives more than her body. You don't just hire a teacher because you read he's slept with a lot of beautiful women."

"I don't see why not. Especially since I know from experience just how good you are."

His grip tightened, and he turned her so that she faced him. "Amy, Amy. I like you just the way you are. I don't want to be the one to change or corrupt you."

"This is *my* idea, not yours. I was a bookworm in school. I believe in lessons and study, and now I want to study…sex!"

"Don't be ridiculous!"

As the wind whipped her hair, he slowly brought his

long, tapered fingers to her cheek. "Go back inside before you're blown into this pool, and I'll forget we ever had this idiotic conversation."

"Why shouldn't we?" She circled his waist with his arm and pulled him to her. "You want Château Serene, and I want you. Or rather, what you can teach me."

When she stood on tiptoe and leaned toward him, he took a quick breath. With a shaking hand she stroked his cheek and then his lips. He stiffened. For a moment longer he stood motionless. Then as if drawn by an irresistible force, he slowly bent his head and kissed her, sending wild shards of sensation to every nerve ending in her body.

"You're good," she whispered breathlessly, pressing herself against him. "The best. That's why I'm choosing you."

"It's called chemistry. It's because I like you and you like me. But you're the last woman I'd ever choose as my mistress."

"Ouch!"

"I meant that as a compliment. Trust me. It would be more dangerous for you than you think. You've read about the women I've hurt. Women always want more than I can give. I always walk. I'm not capable of the kind of love and commitment people like you need. I was abandoned young, so I can be cruel."

"I don't care. All I'm asking for is a few more lessons in bed."

"Dammit, you'll get hurt."

"How, if I have no illusions about how bad you are? How, if I could never love someone as low-down as you? Besides, a sexy bad guy has to sleep with someone. Why not me? Especially since you'll get Château Serene for your trouble. If you're cruel, why do you care?"

A bolt of lightning crashed near the pool, the stark, white blaze lighting the grounds and his scowling face.

"Do we have a deal or not?" she asked softly.

"Who else will you make this offer to if I don't accept? I should call your mother," he said in a low, seething tone. "And tell her you need somebody to watch over you while you're here."

"Why can't that be you?"

His dark eyes stared straight into hers. Then he went still, and she saw something of his real desire.

"Go! Run!" he growled.

"No!"

"All right. Have it your way."

He scooped her into his arms, and his mouth came down hard on her lips, her throat, her breasts, causing her blood to heat and her heart to pulse like a drum. Then he hauled her into the house.

Once they were in the kitchen, he wrapped her in his arms. Glancing up at her aunt's calendar on the wall, she said, "In one month, at this hour, I'll sign your contract." Pushing loose from his tight embrace, she grabbed a red pencil and circled the date.

"As if I give a damn right now," he said. "The important thing is that after one month with me you'll be so sure you're sexy, you'll never question yourself again."

"You swear? On a hundred Bibles?"

"This isn't a child's game." Leaning down, he caught her bottom lip with his teeth and tugged gently. Then his tongue invaded her mouth.

A long time later he said, "Who's making up our first lesson plan?"

"You! You're the teacher, *mon amour*."

He pulled his mobile phone out of his pocket and turned it off. Then he kissed her very slowly until his heart was thudding and his breath was rough.

"Strip," he said, his voice hoarse and low as he let her go.

"While you just stand there and watch me...like I'm some woman you're appraising in a brothel?" Startled, she backed away from him an inch or two.

"You're my mistress. I want to see you naked. It's your job to satisfy my wishes."

"You think I'll be too scared and shy to do it, don't you? You think I'll just sell the vineyard without...you having to live up to our bargain?"

"If you have a grain of sense, dammit, yes!"

"Then I guess it's up to me to show you once and for all that I'm dead serious about being a satisfactory mistress."

Her hands went to her ears and she plucked her pearl earrings off, one by one. Next she removed her pearl necklace. Then she began to unbutton her gauzy white dress, touching herself and sighing as she did so.

When the soft fabric slid down her erect nipples and thighs and pooled at her feet, she felt feverishly warm, even though she wore nothing but the transparent white thong panties he'd watched her blushingly buy at Camden.

She moved toward him and boldly traced her fingers over his shoulders, down his broad back. She cupped his hips, his thighs and, last of all, his erection. His entire body was hot. He was fully aroused.

"Am I beautiful?" she whispered. "I do so want to be beautiful for you."

With a groan, his arms wrapped her close. His mouth sought hers in a long, demanding kiss that made her body tighten and quiver.

"Yes, dammit, you're beautiful."

Lifting her gently, he carried her through the house to her bedroom.

Seven

A callused fingertip ran the length of her body in the velvet dark. Only dimly did she hear the rain beating against the stone walls and roof tiles and racing off the roof into the gutters. Blasts of lightning shot the night with fire. Not that she could see much blindfolded. And only vaguely was she aware of the bursts of thunder.

"They say that the blind are more sensitive to touch," he'd whispered when he'd locked her in her bedroom.

Amy's eyes were still covered by a strip of black silk. She was naked, and her arms were stretched above her head and tied loosely with a long, white, silken scarf. Why had she let him tie her up?

Why not? He was the teacher. This was his lesson plan.

"If you're going to be sexy, we must break down your inhibitions. You must be wild and free and willing to try things you've never tried," he'd told her.

"Like making love in the rain out by the pool."

"If the lightning stops," he promised.

Her ankles were wide apart and tied by scarves at each corner of the bed. His head was lodged between her open thighs, his tongue tracing silky, satin circles and delving deeply inside her, tasting her essence.

For an hour she'd lain helplessly beneath him as his mouth and tongue had roamed her body, licking the soles of her feet and between her toes, licking her in the most intimate places until she'd become a wanton, quivering mass of flaming female sensation. When she cried out, feeling hot, on the edge, ready to explode beneath his next kiss or flick of his tongue, he slowed his exquisite torture.

"Don't stop. Please," she begged.

"Anticipation," he murmured, kissing her secret femininity, "is everything. Sex is mainly in the mind, you know."

"You're killing me."

He eased himself higher along her body. "No, I'm loving you. I want you to know how totally, how completely sexy you are." He kissed her temple and she quivered. Then he gently kissed her lips. "You are the most responsive woman I've ever known."

"But I'm afraid."

"I won't hurt you. Though sometimes a little fear enhances the thrill."

"Kiss me. Hold me," she pleaded.

His mouth found hers. Their lips and tongues joined, tasted. In utter bliss at the taste of him, she sighed. He settled down on top of her, his hips aligning themselves over hers before he slowly entered her.

His skin was even wetter and hotter than her own as

he hovered above her, barely moving, each stroke expert. Suddenly he plunged harder, and she was screaming and weeping. When she began to writhe, he exploded. With a cry, she tore the scarves loose, and her hands clutched his shoulders.

"Yes," she whispered, wrapping her legs around his waist and arching herself upward. "Yes."

He buried himself even more deeply when she shuddered and dug her nails into his back.

Afterward, as he lay on top of her, his shaft still buried inside her, she reveled in the utter completeness she felt to be thus joined to him and held by him.

She'd missed him so much. How was that possible?

He kissed her brow, her cheeks, her eyelids and lashes, even the tip of her nose, muttering low, sweet words in French that she only partially understood.

"You could be insulting me and I'd never know."

"You'd know. And I'm not insulting you."

"I didn't think you were."

His stomach grumbled.

"Hungry?" she whispered.

"You did say dinner at eight o'clock sharp? And even for a Provençal, we're long past that hour."

"Oh, yes, dinner." She got up slowly. "And I was thinking about making love in the rain."

"With a mind like that you damn sure don't need me to touch you to be sexy."

"Oh, but I do."

They dressed, and he followed her into the kitchen where he surprised her by proving that he could be as useful behind the stove as in her bed.

Together they chopped fresh vegetables and made pizza—or rather, three pizzas, mushroom, cheese and anchovy. He tossed a salad while she put the finishing touches on a steaming casserole of roasted chicken and mushrooms that she'd prepared earlier.

After lingering over dinner and sharing a crème caramel, she thought he would surely leave. Instead, he stayed to help her wash and put away the dishes. She turned out the lights and locked up. When they reached the front door, instead of stepping outside so she could lock it, he took her hand and led her outside into the mist.

"You said you wanted to make love in the rain," he reminded her.

She shook her head. "Not now."

"How about a quickie?"

"I don't think I could."

"A sexy girl's got to have a quickie lesson." He pushed her against a cool stone wall, stripped off her jeans, unzipped his and penetrated her. His dark eyes glowed with intense black heat as he thrust into her again and again.

Slam. Bam. Instantly she was aflame. Why hadn't she thought she wanted this? She held on to him, begging, clinging, wanting all of him.

"Condom," she whispered several strokes later.

"Damn."

"Damn," she agreed as he withdrew.

Panting hard, he stood before her.

"Wait here," he finally managed between hoarse breaths.

Gasping too, pushing her hair out of her eyes, she nodded. "As if I could go anywhere."

When he returned, he kissed her tenderly on the brow and eyelids and lips before shoving himself inside her again. As before, his movements were hard and fast. For long, glorious moments her body strained with his. She screamed at the exact moment he clutched her shoulders and drove into her with a final shudder.

When her knees buckled, he pulled her close. "Wrap those legs around my waist."

When she did as he asked, he walked with her inside the house and slammed the door.

"You're a quick study. I don't think you need a month of lessons, *chérie.*"

"That's not our deal," she whispered.

She thought he would say goodbye and go. Instead, he carried her back to her bedroom where they slept wrapped in each other's arms just as they had in London.

Only, the next morning when she awoke to brilliant sunshine and that delicious soreness between her thighs, his black head was on the pillow beside hers. Snuggling closer to his warm body, she smiled. How nice he felt. How right. How pleasant it would be to have him always.

Her eyes snapped wide open. As she stared at his furred chest, her heart pounded.

His long lashes fluttered lazily open.

"One month?" he murmured. "You look like you're having second thoughts. You sure you really want so much of me?"

"One month," she insisted. No way could she confess the depth of the terrifying tenderness she felt for him.

"Usually my affairs never last that long."

She swallowed. His comment hurt, more than it should have.

"So, this will be a growth experience for you, too," she said, attempting a lightness she didn't feel.

He frowned as if something was bothering him, too. Was he already tired of her?

"So far I have no complaints," he said. "It's been fun."

"For me, too," she agreed even though she suddenly felt miserable.

When she got up, he lay on his back with his arms crossed under his head and his dark, brilliant eyes watching everything she did. Taking her time, she put on a soft, pink cotton dress that had faded from red. Slowly, self-consciously, she braided her hair.

What was he thinking as she used a pencil to darken her eyebrows and a tube of lipstick to make her mouth redder? Was he bored? Did he think she was using him? Did he feel resentful? She would give anything to know. But she did not have a right to his thoughts.

She had rights only to his body. And only for one month.

When she was dressed, she asked him what he wanted for breakfast.

"I know a café in the village."

"Won't everyone know about us then? Even your family?"

"Probably. The villagers are terrible gossips. Especially about the de Fourniers. But they know I want to buy your vineyard. If we bring the contract, perhaps we can fool them into thinking we're conducting business."

"With your reputation?"

"You're leaving. Do you really mind if they suspect you're my mistress?"

When she shook her head, a slow, possessive grin spread

across his face. If she hadn't known better she might have believed he wanted everyone to know she was his.

"But what about you, your sisters and your mother? Your mother could barely stand talking to me the other day. You know how much she disliked my aunt."

"Don't worry about my family," he muttered, pulling her close and kissing her. "I'll deal with them."

With the top of his Alfa Romeo down, he sped down the slick, narrow roads that climbed through the fields of lavender to the red-roofed, medieval village perched on a cliff.

He drove so fast her thick braid whipped her face, and tires screamed around the curves. She should have expected speed from him and recklessness. Not that rubber ever veered once off the asphalt. Nor did he come too close to the cyclists on the edge of the road.

The car was nimble, his concentration complete, his expertise profound. He knew the road, the car and his abilities, and soon, instead of fear, she felt exhilaration.

She'd never been in a car with butter-soft leather seats like this, in a car with a driver who could make her feel like she was flying in bed and out of it.

"So what kind of car is this?"

"A '67 Duetto Spider."

"It's cute."

"Cute." He snorted. "It was the best damn sports car made that year. Not that it ever caught on—even after starring in a major film. Did you ever see *The Graduate?*"

She shook her head.

"Someday soon we'll have to watch it together."

He slowed when they reached the village, which was

crowded because it was market day. He cruised the narrow, winding lanes overflowing with haphazardly positioned stalls that sold all kinds of wares. Young gypsy women in tight bustiers and shiny skirts ran up to the Alfa Romeo, shaking long plaits of garlic and lemons in Amy's face.

When she reached for them, he said, "No shopping," and kept driving until he found a parking space near a fountain two blocks from his favorite café. "I'm starving."

As they got out, the clock tower chimed. He took her hand, and they walked up the hill past galleries and benches that would have been perfect for people-watching. Everywhere there were stalls selling everything from olives and fresh bread to terrines and Disney toys.

He tugged on her hand when she edged toward a yellow-and-white canopy. "No shopping," he reminded her.

"But he's selling fresh croissants."

"We're nearly at the café."

Two minutes later they were seated on a rooftop terrace under an arbor dripping bougainvillea. He laid the contract on their table, and then they ignored it and chatted until their omelets laced with pungent truffles arrived. The food was so delicious they ate in silence. No sooner had he finished his and was sipping café au lait when his mobile rang.

He fished the phone out of his pocket only to frown when he saw who it was.

"Sorry. It's my mother. I had my phone turned off until a few minutes ago. I guess I'd better talk to her."

Amy nodded.

"*Bonjour.*" After this brief greeting, he was soon scowling. "You shouldn't have done that," he said in sharp, staccato French. His gaze on Amy, he listened with increasing irritation. "You're right," he snapped. "I'll be there as soon as I can."

He flipped the phone shut and jammed it back in his pocket.

"Let me guess. She knows we're together and she's not pleased?"

"Gossip travels fast. She didn't fall for the contract on the table, and she's not happy I didn't return to the château last night. Apparently she'd made plans—"

"I knew we shouldn't have eaten in such a public establishment so early in the morning."

"My personal life is none of her business."

"She's your mother."

"I'm thirty-five. The trouble is she's always been able to dictate to my sisters. She failed miserably with my father, and her schemes frequently annoy the hell out of me."

He stared up at the impressive Château de Fournier, which topped the highest hill above the village, and then fell into a gloomy silence.

Amy knew his family had lived there for hundreds of years. Once she'd told her aunt it must be wonderful to belong to a family with such ancient roots and traditions like the de Fourniers.

"They're ridiculously conservative," Aunt Tate had replied. "His first wife was so out of touch with the modern world, she drove him into my arms."

Amy looked at Remy. "Surely if you tell your mother you're merely seeing me because you're negotiating the sale of the vineyard, she'll be more understanding," she began.

"The last thing I intend to do is discuss our relationship. Not with her. Or anyone else."

"I know you were trying to improve your relations with your family, and I don't want to be a problem."

Remy's hand closed over hers. "No problem. At least it won't be after today." Squeezing her fingers, he lifted them to his lips.

Seeing the tender gesture, the proprietor winked at Amy and made a pleased little bow before darting back inside.

A short while later the man reappeared, beaming. Remy held up his hand for the check. Grinning widely, the owner zoomed over and slapped it on top the contract.

As if still preoccupied by the phone call, Remy did not attempt to make conversation with the man or with her. As soon as he paid, he led her out onto the street to find his car.

Rocks crunching beneath their shoes, they walked in silence. Despite Remy's mood, Amy was enjoying the brightness of the sun, the vivid red geraniums and the sweetness of the lavender as they topped the hill in search of the Alfa Romeo.

Just as they reached it, she heard a roar, and a green Renault careened straight at them. Swerving almost into Remy the driver hit the brakes at the last minute. Jumping out of the way, Remy grabbed Amy and circled her with his arms protectively.

Yelling Remy's name, the driver charged out of the Renault like a bull.

The solid fellow looked tough enough to do real damage even though he barely came up to Remy's shoulder. He wore rough, faded work clothes, and his blue eyes burned so hotly Amy wondered if he'd already been drinking.

"Murderer! You think you're smart because they let

you off? You think your money can buy anything, even justice for my son's death!"

"I'm as sorry about André as you are, Maurice."

"You! You don't know anything!"

Maurice held up a fist. Then he took a step backward and slammed it down on the hood of the Alfa Romeo with so much force he dented it. He began to hurl further abuse at Remy, making violent hand gestures as he did so. His vernacular French was not entirely comprehensible to Amy, but Remy turned so pale she began to tremble.

White-lipped, Remy grabbed Amy's arm. Leading her around to the passenger side of the car, he yanked her door open and said, "Get in."

When he raced back around to the driver's side, Maurice hurled himself at Amy's window.

He spat heavily on the ground. "Stupid girl! You should have nothing to do with this man. He killed my son! He's dangerous! He hurts everybody he touches—especially women! He drives like a maniac!"

Remy strode back around the car. "Maurice, you'd better leave her alone."

"Or what? You'll call the police? You think you're safe because you own this town, don't you."

"If you want to talk to me, make an appointment with my secretary." Remy held out a business card. "I'll be happy to see you anytime."

Maurice grabbed it and shredded it, then hurled the bits at Remy. He spat on the ground again. "I'll see you in hell. That's where I'll see you."

"Fine." Remy got into his car, slammed the door and jammed his key in the ignition. The engine roared to life.

Careful of Maurice, whose bulk was blocking half the

lane, Remy shifted and drove up on the curb to avoid the man and get away. Only when they were outside the village did he speed up, but his face remained grim. He gripped the wheel so hard, his knuckles punched the skin like bleached bones.

Even when the village was several miles behind them, his fury, grief and self-loathing remained such a presence in the car that Amy grew close to tears. What must he have suffered this past year?

"Are you cold?" he asked her. "Do you want the top up?"

She pushed her braid back. "No, I'm fine."

"Right." Jamming his foot down on the accelerator, he sped toward Château Serene as if chased by demons.

She thought he wanted to be rid of her so he could be alone. But when he pulled up in the curving stone drive of Château Serene and stopped, he reached across her to open her door.

"I wish I could have spared you that little scene," he said.

"I'm okay."

He drew a deep, resigned breath. For the next few minutes he was silent. "Look, if you've changed your mind…about seeing me for a month, I'll understand."

She buried her face in her hands and shook her head.

"I can't see you until tomorrow. Apparently I have a previous engagement today."

"Oh." Looking up, she fought to hide her disappointment. Not that she asked questions. He had a life.

His jaw was set. His expression was so dark and cold, her eyes began to burn. Determined to escape before she broke down completely, she quickly scooted toward her open door. But when she would have gotten out, his arm snaked across the back of the seat and pulled her to him.

"You're not crying, are you?"

"No!" When she felt dampness oozing down her cheeks, she sniffed. "Sinuses. I'm allergic to the cypresses."

"Liar." He crushed her to him, stroking her face and hair. "I'm sorry. I had a great time until my mother called and Maurice showed up. I'll miss you today." He kissed each cheek, tasting her hot, salty tears. "What will you do with all your free time?"

"Pack."

"You're sweet. I don't deserve you," he whispered. Then he let her go.

She got out slowly and walked hurriedly up the drive. Before she reached her door, he was roaring away.

She would have waved if he'd ever once looked back. Since he didn't, she watched the Alfa Romeo until it disappeared over the first hill.

Where was he going? Who would he spend the rest of the day with?

She opened her door and walked into her dark, empty house that without him, seemed colder and gloomier than a tomb. She'd been his mistress for only one night and already he felt like a dangerous obsession.

If she were smart, she'd call his agent and agree to sell immediately.

Eight

Remembering it was market day, Remy parked the car in a shady alley beneath the château. He opened the car door and then closed it again. For a long time he sat hunched over the steering wheel, staring at the ancient stone wall.

Mistress for a month? What the hell was he doing? Hadn't he sworn to quit focusing on what he wanted without thinking of the consequences for others?

An affair with him was not in Amelia's best interests. With women like her, sex was a messy business. She might say no strings in the beginning, but she wouldn't even remember the bargain once her emotions started complicating matters.

But what if she was right, and he succeeded in making her believe she was a sexy femme fatale? Just the thought of her doing the things that she was doing with him now with her Hawaiian beach bum, made his gut clench.

Fisting his hand, he shoved his door open and angrily flung himself up the lane toward the château. Fifteen minutes of climbing had him standing beneath the famous lion carved above the lintel. Glancing up, he saw his mother and Céline in a high window. Céline's back was to him, but his mother's gaze, cold and fixed, was on him. She'd been watching him for some time.

On the phone she'd said she'd invited Céline down for a few days. The problem was she hadn't seen the need to inform him. Dreading straightening out the mess she'd created, he bolted up the wide stone stairs that angled twice before climbing even higher.

The last thing he wanted to do was offend Céline. But he'd committed to Amelia's bargain, so the next thirty days were hers.

He would have preferred to confront his mother first, but long before he reached the portal and the ornate doors with their bronze knocker, he heard high heels clicking much too rapidly on stone for the person who approached to be his sedate mother.

When he rounded a curve, Céline ran toward him. Her face alight, she looked gorgeous in a simple white dress and white sandals with laces around her slim ankles. Her golden hair, tied back by a white satin ribbon, bounced about her shoulders.

"Remy!"

Blue eyes locked on his face. How flushed and perfect she was in the lemony light. If only he wasn't involved with Amelia, he might have been happy to see her.

"I feel so terrible," she began, gushing concern. "I just realized that maybe your mother hadn't told you I was coming. You have other plans for the weekend, don't you?"

"I'm negotiating the purchase of Château Serene."

"I see."

"I'll call you in…say, a month or so."

"I've waited this long. I guess I can wait a little longer."

"You always were more patient than I."

"A month from now. I'll write it on my calendar," she said gaily, reminding him of Amelia circling the same date with her red pencil on her calendar.

"Since we're such old friends, I'll be blunter than I probably should be…Your mother has hinted that…she has certain fond hopes."

"She's always liked you, so I can well imagine her hopes. I was not opposed to them until…like I said, this…er…other business obligation developed."

"Château Serene? For exactly a month?" she murmured. Her eyes were filled with questions before he looked away.

Remy's interview with his mother the next morning in the grand salon was difficult, especially after he mentioned his need to go to Cannes to oversee the renovation of the family villa and his desire to invite Amelia to go with him.

Wearing black silk and diamonds, Alexis de Fournier looked like a countess from another era as she stood under the gigantic crystal-and-gold chandelier, studying her son with cold, calculating eyes.

"You can't possibly be serious about taking that conniving little witch of a niece to our home in Cannes."

"I will take her, if she'll accept my invitation," Remy stated bluntly.

"How can you be so stupid? Not to mention blind? She's Tate all over again. Simply everybody is in Cannes right now. People will see you with her."

"So?"

"She's trying to catch you in a weak moment."

"How well you seem to know her. Have you even met her?"

"All your sisters agree with me."

"Why do you always have to involve them?"

"They are brilliant women. And they want the best for you."

"Spare me their concern. I never interfere in their lives. Did you ask for my help with Château Serene or not?"

"Yes, but I didn't mean for you to—"

"Be happy, then. In this I am giving you your way. I promise you that in one month Miss Weatherbee will be gone, and you'll have your precious Château Serene all to yourself. When and *if* I feel like it, I will call Céline and invite her down for a long weekend, and we'll see how it goes. No promises, though. Until then, I belong to Miss Weatherbee."

"This is absurd. Why should you have to spend so much time with her? Is this just because she doesn't know anybody else?"

"I enjoy her."

"What could you possibly have in common with a…a shop girl? Why do you always have to be so difficult?"

"Maybe because I'm your son."

"You attack me just like your father used to."

"Which father—Montoya or the *comte?*"

A flush swept her neck and cheek, but she refused to be distracted. "Remy, I'm sure she has designs on you just like Tate had on your father."

"That's untrue."

"How do you know?"

"For one thing she read and believed the terrible tabloid

stories about me. For another she is nothing like Tate. She is naive, shy…"

His mother's eyes narrowed. "Shy? Naive? *Remy!* Listen to yourself. I haven't heard you talk about a woman like this…maybe ever. This woman arouses tender, protective feelings in you. I don't believe she could if she thought you were vicious and treated you accordingly. Quite the contrary. I am more convinced than ever she's after you."

"I won't hear any more."

"I want to know exactly what is going on between the two of you. Young, ambitious women can be very manipulative when they want a man. Very charming. Oh, Remy, I thought the worst thing you'd ever do was drive those horrible cars that reminded me of…"

"Montoya?"

Her face went the deep, dead purple of an overripe grape. "Do you have to say his name? I—I regret him. He ruined my life."

"And me? Do you regret me?"

"Of course not! You'll never know what I went through during each race you drove," she continued when she'd regained a small bit of her composure. "But this is worse. I will never speak to you again if you allow a serious attachment to develop between yourself and Tate's niece. *Never.* Do I make myself understood?"

"Perfectly. You can be stubborn. So can I. I refuse to discuss my relationship with Miss Weatherbee with you again. Do I make *myself* understood?"

When she didn't reply, he said, "I need to check the train schedules to make sure Céline's train to Paris is on time."

"What? She won't be staying? You two won't be—"

"You heard me." He turned on his heel.

"Remy!"

Without looking back, he kept walking down the great hall.

"Remy!"

Amelia was happily enjoying the glorious morning with its bright blue sky. She walked briskly along the road edged on both sides by perfumed clumps of lavender. Lebanese cedars cast long shadows over the road. The air smelled of cedar and pine and lavender and freshly mown grasses. She was thinking that even though she hadn't heard from Remy in nearly twenty-four hours, he'd promised to see her today. So when she saw his red sports car zooming toward her, her heart leaped with pure joy.

Remy! She ran out into the middle of the road waving wildly to flag him down.

He'd hit the brakes long before she saw the beautiful blonde beside him. The woman, with her creamy skin and glamorous silk beige jacket, was even more beautiful than Carol.

Immediately Amy felt like her ugly-duckling self. Why had she worn her oldest and baggiest pair of jeans with the holes in the knees and a faded shirt that wasn't even all that clean? Why hadn't she at least put on lipstick?

When he pulled alongside her, he said, "Hi there, neighbor," as if she were no more than a casual acquaintance.

Sucking in a sharp little breath, Amelia tried to appear casual and uninterested.

"I saw you waving. Did you have a breakdown? Do you need a ride somewhere?" he asked.

The blonde's icy blue eyes narrowed as they raked Amelia. Her shapely, glossy-pink mouth thinned before she looked away.

Judged and found lacking.

Amelia felt stricken. If she'd been in her ugly-duckling mode when the gorgeous pair had driven up, she was definitely in an acute stress molt now.

"Oh, I was just taking a walk before it got too hot," she said, feeling desperate to escape them.

"I want you to meet an old friend. I'm driving her to the station. Céline, this is Amelia Weatherbee."

Céline barely glanced at her. She was clearly anxious to be on her way with Remy.

He nodded to Amy. "Well, if I can't give you a lift, enjoy your walk."

"The day is so lovely, how could I do otherwise?" she muttered, her voice so soft it was almost inaudible.

"See you later, then." He tossed her a careless smile before hitting the gas.

Hugging herself tightly, she watched the Alfa Romeo until it was no more than a blurry red dot against the horizon. Then she bit her lips, squared her shoulders and cut directly across the vineyard toward the château. An hour later she was inside the house alone packing furiously when she heard the Alfa Romeo roar up her drive.

Remy killed the engine and knocked. When she didn't answer he banged more loudly and began shouting her name.

Squeezing her eyes shut and pressing her throbbing

temples, she held her breath. How could he think she'd want to see him this morning? When his banging grew even louder, she hugged herself and began rocking back and forth.

When the front door slammed open, she jumped. Calling her name, he stomped through the rooms looking for her.

"Go home, why don't you!" she yelled. "I'm busy!"

"So, *here* you are!" He grinned at her from the doorway. "I knew you'd be angry. That's why I came as soon as I could."

She yanked a pink ballerina figurine off the shelf and pretended she couldn't decide whether to pack it in the box for the antique dealer or the one for her mother.

"Well?" he said when she just stood with her hands frozen around the slim porcelain legs. "Whatever you do, don't throw it. Not at me, anyway!"

"As if I'd waste a valuable porcelain on the likes of you! You are so not worth it!"

He laughed. "Don't be mad."

"You think I'm jealous, don't you? Well, I'm not!"

"Did I say the j-word?"

She set the ballerina down on a low table for fear that she might throw it at him. "I'm not!"

"Of course you're not." His voice was mild. Was he teasing her? "I'm just the scoundrel you chose to be your sex teacher. You couldn't possibly have feelings for me."

"Right. And you certainly don't have to account to me for every second you spend with someone else! I don't care who you're with! Or where you go! And I won't ever!"

"Excellent. You are the perfect mistress for a man like me. We have a rational arrangement, and you made the rules."

He stepped forward and picked up the ballerina and turned it thoughtfully in his hands. "So as a rational person, aren't you even the slightest bit curious to know more about her?"

"No!"

"Well, just in case you're a little bit curious, she's an old friend."

"Define friend. No! I said I don't care, and I don't."

He smiled. "We dated years ago. Before I was the kind of man who stars in tabloid newspapers. She's a Parisian fashion designer and the widow of a German prince."

He couldn't possibly know that she'd once dreamed of designing clothes. And what was she doing, instead? Recycling used clothes.

"My mother and sisters adore her." He set the ballerina back down and knelt beside Amy. "They all agree she's perfect for me."

"I don't care who she is or what she is or what she is or was to you!"

"Right. Well, since you're not the least bit jealous or curious, I commend you. But the fact remains that she came to Provence to see me. But because of you, I sent her away. I made her and my mother unhappy. And now I'm sort of at loose ends."

"Not my problem."

"Who demanded to be my mistress for a month?" he queried in a goaded undertone. Standing up, he took her hands and pulled her up beside him. "I am in need of a woman. Are you up to the job or not?"

Before she knew what was happening, he'd wrapped his arms around her and was holding her close against the muscular length of his body. Much to her utter amazement, he was fully aroused.

When she placed her hands against his chest to push him away, she felt his violently thudding heart. Had the beautiful Céline turned him on?

"Let me go!" She twisted, using her hands to beat at his shoulders. "I have to pack. I won't be manhandled."

"As my mistress, you do have certain duties," he whispered, gripping her tightly. "Unless you want to resign?"

"No!"

"Good!" Before she could say more, his mouth closed over hers, his tongue hot and seeking.

Foolish person that she was, her heart began to pound and soon she was melting against him.

"Sometimes I hate myself," she murmured.

"For what?" His mouth was nibbling her lips as he tore off his shirt and ripped open his jeans.

"For being so easy. For liking this so much. For wanting you so much."

"For being sexy? Isn't that the whole point of our affair?"

"You talk too much," she said.

"So the hell do you."

She could not wriggle out of her clothes quickly enough.

"Do you want me? Or her?"

He encircled her wrists with his hands and drew her close. "Dammit, who the hell am I with?" he growled. "I told you, my mother invited her. As soon as I saw Céline, I explained that I had other plans and suggested that she take the first train back to Paris. She agreed."

His black head dipped toward hers, reclaiming her mouth.

Was he telling the truth? Amelia didn't know.

She only knew that when he laid her down on the oriental carpet and slid inside her, she'd never wanted anything more than him filling her, completing her, loving her. She was so touched by his return and his ardor and his concern that she might be hurt and jealous, tears leaked out of her eyes as he brushed his mouth down her throat, over her breasts.

Maybe he cared about her feelings, but he did not love her.

And he never would. His coming back meant nothing. They had a business arrangement. That was all.

Not that the true nature of their relationship was easy to remember as his kisses deepened and her senses swirled. And when he made love to her, he swept her away to a new dreamlike reality.

When they could breathe again, he carried her to the bed and began sucking her bottom lip as if he had all the time in the world to make love to her a second time.

"You're not mad at me any longer?" he whispered.

She drew back. "I never was. We will not arouse deep emotions in each other. You will teach, and I will learn."

"And we will both enjoy."

"If only temporarily."

When he caught her closer, her body urged him to take new liberties, even as her heart told her to be cautious.

She was only his mistress for a month. Céline, or someone like her, would win in the end.

"But I have him now," she whispered to herself after her third climax. "I have him now."

"What did you say, *chérie?*" he murmured, his hot breath tickling her ear.

"Nothing important. Nothing the least bit important."

"I believe you have the makings of a perfect mistress. You just get better and better."

Smiling, she lay back. Never had she felt more beautiful.

Nine

Cool, soft moonlight glimmered across the surface of the pool. The night smelled of pine and lavender and starlight.

Remy's manhood was still deeply embedded inside her as she lay beneath him, her naked bottom on the scratchy chaise longue. She sighed, feeling warm and sated from their lovemaking.

With a fingertip he slicked a tendril of her hair back from her hot face. "You work much too hard to be a satisfactory mistress. All those boxes…"

During the past week, she'd packed and organized Aunt Tate's clothes all day, and then every night he'd come and they'd made love, swum and had dinner. She hadn't thought of the beautiful Céline waiting in the wings too often, but when she had, she'd told herself she was just being realistic, that this month with Remy meant nothing beyond her original intention. She was learning to be sexy, and that was all.

"If I'm to leave in a month, I must get certain things done," Amy said, trying to keep her tone casual.

"You said you wanted to be my mistress. I have business in Cannes—a villa in need of some rather extensive repairs. I need to go inspect the job and talk to the engineer. Because of you I've delayed going too long. A real mistress would accompany me."

"Who will pack Aunt Tate's things?"

Caressing her hair with his hands, he kissed her throat, causing her pulse to beat madly.

"Cannes is much too crowded this time of year. Too many English. Too many tourists looking for bargains. Certain friends of mine have told me they'll be there, and that they want to see me. A dutiful mistress would accompany her lover." He lowered his voice. "I swear—the trip would be unbearable without your delightful company."

"That's sweet of you to say."

"What if it's the truth?"

His eyes devoured her features with a fierce hunger she wasn't ready to believe was anything more than sexual interest. After all, they were still hot and naked and wrapped in each other's arms.

"The view is lovely from the villa," he continued. "You need a break. Besides, I'm sick of my mother's silences and dark looks. I'm not used to spending so much time with her. She doesn't ask about you, but you're constantly on her mind."

The cool night wind shivered in the pines before dancing across her hot skin.

"I'm sorry."

"She doesn't like being thwarted. In Cannes, even though it's crowded, we might have some real privacy. Everybody here is her spy."

"Do you really want me all to yourself?"

"Why don't you come and find out?"

She nodded absently as she realized how lonely she'd be without him. Besides, she loved beach towns. But what if some former lover as beautiful as Céline were there to tempt him? Or Céline herself? Amy was startled by how much the thought chilled her.

This wasn't a real romance. It was unwise to feel so possessive, but she couldn't seem to stop herself.

"Good," he said. "Tomorrow, then! Ten o'clock in the morning."

He sounded so thrilled her heart began to pound.

"All right." She grinned, happy that he'd been so determined to take her with him.

He kissed the tip of her nose and slid halfway off her. "Why me?" he murmured so tenderly against her ear that a lump formed in her throat. "Why did you pick me?"

His intense gaze made her heart skip.

Feeling too raw and unsure about revealing her true feelings, she had no choice but to tease him. "Timing I suppose. You just popped into my life when I needed somebody with your skills. All those awful things about you in the newspapers definitely tipped the scales in your favor."

He cursed low in French before adding in a strained tone, "You chose me because you think I'm bad?"

She nodded.

"Well, since I'm training you, I advise that when you're with your next lover, you not be so brutally honest."

"Oh, I won't, I assure you."

She laughed. He didn't.

"Réellement, chérie."

"You aren't like my future lovers or the husband who will father all my soccer players. We both know you're a heartless womanizer—a man without a heart, who's so focused on what he wants, he can't be hurt."

"Right! You've read the papers, so you know me well." Tensing, he eased even farther away from her. Even though his face was in shadow, she could tell his jaw was clenched. Every muscle in his body felt coiled and hard.

"You are becoming like me, even in the short time we've known each other," he said in a controlled tone. "More than you know."

"I don't understand."

"If you weren't like me, you couldn't make love so enthusiastically with a man you can't really care about."

"We both agreed I would be stupid to let myself care about you. This month is about empowerment, not love. You can't possibly understand what it's been like for me. My sister is super-gorgeous. She was always the winner, while I… I just decided not to try—until I met you."

"You think this is a game? Okay, I won't argue. You have your opinion and I have mine."

"Then why are you suddenly so angry?"

"Dammit, who's angry?"

Abruptly he jumped off the chaise longue, strode to the pool and dived into the deep end. As he swam rapid laps, the moonlight glittered across the bunched, muscular curves of his tanned arms.

She sat up. Somewhere in the forest, a lone nightingale broke into song. Feeling chilled, Amy wrapped herself in a towel. The longer she watched him, the more awkward and rejected she felt.

Why was he so angry? Had she hurt him? Surely not.

Why did she care so much that she might have hurt him? Or that he thought she was as bad as *he* was?

He was wrong. She wasn't like him. No matter what, she would stick to her plan.

It was becoming more and more difficult for Amy to pretend that she could be with Remy and not come to care about him.

Constantly she reminded herself that he wanted only one thing from her, Château Serene, just as she wanted only one thing from him—sexual confidence. She'd made the rules for their relationship. Now all she had to do was live by them.

So knowing all this, she shouldn't be so excited about going to Cannes that she spent half the night packing for the trip. She'd choose an outfit, lay the pieces out on the bed and eye them critically before trying them on. Then she'd work endlessly with her shoes, jewelry and purses, only to discard her selections in a heap and run to the closet and yank more things out. Nothing seemed right. She grabbed some sleep and then resumed packing in the morning. She was still at it when she heard his Alfa Romeo in her drive.

When he saw all the fancy clothes strewn about her aunt's bedroom, he laughed.

"You're overthinking this. It's hot. The sun is bright and burning. Braid your hair. Wear sunglasses. Pack a bathing suit and sunscreen and shorts."

"But won't we go out at night?"

"Throw in a dress."

"You're a man. Which means you think you know everything even when you're clueless."

She ordered him to wait in the garden while she finished, and he did. Only, he drove her mad by yelling, "Are you ready yet?" about every ten minutes.

And she drove *him* mad by yelling back, "You're not helping."

Finally they were in his car jammed in between all the other cars and trucks clogging the highway that went south to the Riviera.

"Looks like everybody and his dog is going to Cannes," Remy said.

Despite the traffic the drive down was fun. They talked and laughed and sang along with the radio.

"I usually hate the drive," he said. "But with a proper mistress to amuse me, it's not half bad."

She didn't admit that she'd never had half so much fun in a car with anyone. Before she knew it, the gates of his magnificent, rustic, limestone, hilltop villa swung open, and a guard in a brown uniform waved them inside.

They drove past a swimming pool and sunbathing terraces. Then Remy braked in front of the villa, and a servant came running out to help them unpack. No sooner had their luggage been placed on racks in the grandest suite of the villa than Remy led her from room to room as eagerly as a boy, showing her dazzling, panoramic views of a city that reminded her a little of Waikiki.

Holding her hand, he named the glittering hotels and beaches. Then he pointed out the palm trees, crystal-blue water and distant islands. He was so attentive and the surroundings so beautiful she felt like pinching herself to make sure it was real.

But it wasn't real. They were playing a game. Why was it becoming so hard to remember that he didn't really care about her? And that she couldn't let herself be foolish enough to care, either?

"The villa is yours?" she asked, pulling her hand free of his.

"The family's. We share it."

"Have you brought other women here?" she asked, and then steeled herself for his answer.

"You mean other mistresses? *Real* mistresses?" His dark eyes flashed. "Jealous?"

"Sorry for the questions. None of my business."

"Would it be so terrible if we treated each other like real human beings?"

When she couldn't answer, he watched her for a long moment. "Right. You could never care about a man like me who's done all the terrible things I've done."

"Which is good," she said with false gaiety, "because my heart is safe with such a man."

She tried to move away toward a window, but he seized her hand and pulled her closer. "Is it?"

In vain she struggled to twist free of him.

"Is that all that matters to you—being safe?" He took her hand and lifted it to his lips. "Why did you ask me to make you your mistress if you didn't want a little danger?"

At his dark look or maybe because his kisses against her wrist made her heart leap, she began to tremble. When he stopped kissing her and watched her face as if hanging on her next words, she wondered what he was hoping for—that she'd prove herself to be a little idiot and beg him to love her?

She stiffened and said nothing.

"All right, I'll stop," he said.

A gloom fell over him and he was silent for a while. Not that he let his bad mood linger for long. As if determined to make her happy, he took her hand and showed her the rest of the house, and when they returned to the bedroom, he pulled her into his arms again.

"Those other women…you should forget them. I have. They don't matter to me anymore. In fact, that life matters less and less to me. *You* matter. More than I bargained for."

"I—I can't let myself believe that."

"Why the hell not?"

"You're a *comte*. Those other women, they were so beautiful. Céline is even more beautiful."

"*Chérie,* haven't I taught you anything? You are a darling, precious woman. Sexier than hell, too. You don't fake anything. You're just you. Your hair doesn't come out of a bottle. When you laugh or kiss or hold me, you mean it."

"My nails are fake."

"*You're* real." He pulled her closer and held her fiercely, his dark eyes blazing, his heart thudding, and soon her own heart beat with equal violence.

In spite of her jealousy of those beautiful women both in his past and in his future, she began to burn for him with a consuming need that was all too real.

She stroked his cheek, kissed him greedily, and then let her tongue slide between his lips. One taste of him had her breathless and aching for more.

He cupped her chin. Breathing as hard and fast as she was, he tightened his arms around her body.

More than anything she wanted to make him forget all the others, at least while she was with him. Her kisses and exploring fingertips became white-hot. She poured her soul into every caress, into every feather-light kiss. He was equally ferocious and needy. His kisses were so ardent and scorchingly intimate, he swept her away, and she wondered what he might need to prove.

They made love violently on the enormous bed and then tenderly in the gold-trimmed marble shower. Afterward she clung to him, breathing hard, while his hands and lips continued to caress her with such reverence and hunger she felt totally adored. Which made no sense. Still, she turned her wet head, snuggling closer against his hot, tanned shoulder, her pulse beating faster than it should have.

"You're a good teacher," she whispered, trying to lighten the mood.

"Is that all you think that was?" His voice and eyes were dark and hard. "Sex lessons well learned from an experienced teacher? Dammit!" He jerked free of her.

"Remy!"

He slammed out of the shower and snapped a towel off the rack.

Cold air rushed into the shower, chilling her.

Whipping the towel around his waist, he charged out of the bathroom.

"Remy!"

He didn't answer or return.

She laid her head against the cold, wet marble as steam seeped out of the shower.

She felt desperately unhappy, and she couldn't bear to think why.

Ten

Too furious to call his engineer or even to dress, Remy stormed to the bar. Floor-to-ceiling glass windows revealed an expansive view of Cannes. Dark clouds were sweeping across the Mediterranean. Not that Remy gave much thought to the view or the weather.

He grabbed a crystal glass and splashed scotch into it so recklessly the liquor sloshed all over his hands.

Hard liquor on an empty stomach. Before dinner. He was drinking like an American.

He bolted the shot, grimaced against its fire and his fierce need for more of the same. He picked the bottle up and then put it down. Shoving his glass away, he turned from the bar.

Damn her! He remembered rolling with her on the big bed, their legs and arms entwined, his mouth sucking and licking all her secret satiny places until she quivered and moaned. He shuddered as he recalled how good she'd felt when he'd thrust inside her that final time. No woman had ever felt half so good, so hot or moist, so tight or wildly responsive. God, she was sweet.

She's playing a silly game, and you're her toy, you fool. The trouble is you're not playing. Not anymore.

She'd made it very clear she was using him. He had to get a grip. He knew too well what it was like for life to take a dark turn, and for mistakes to become irreparable.

He wouldn't make another one.

He wasn't falling in love with her.

He wasn't that stupid.

This was about sex. That was all she wanted, so it couldn't be about anything else.

Amy was leaning toward the brilliantly lit mirror with an eyebrow pencil cocked above the curve of her eyebrow, when Remy knocked.

She started. "Come in."

The door opened. Instantly her hand began to shake so badly she had to put the pencil down. Only, her hand moved too jerkily, and the pencil spun onto the floor and rolled across the polished marble straight at him.

Leaning down, he picked it up. He stood up slowly, tension radiating from him as he slowly set it on the counter.

"You look nice," she said, noting his dark jacket and slacks.

When he said nothing she picked up the pencil and rushed to fill the awkward silence with words.

"Did you make your calls?" she asked.

"No. I had a stiff drink. Then I went for a short run. Nothing like the miracle of booze and endorphins to improve one's mood."

She smiled. His attempt to do the same was fleeting and tense.

"You were fast, too," she whispered. "Much faster than me."

"Take all the time you need. I still have to call my engineer and the architect. When you're ready, I'll take you out. Oh, and dress up. We'll eat somewhere fancy, and maybe later we'll dance. Or if you prefer to gamble, there are two casinos where we might run into friends, and I can show you off."

She would have preferred to stay in the villa with him, but perhaps being alone with him wasn't the best idea. She felt too vulnerable and needy, too much her real self. And despite his run, he seemed edgy.

After he left, she went into the bedroom and opened her suitcase, rummaging through it until she found the flirty red dress and silver shoes she'd worn in London. She spread them on the rumpled sheets where they'd recently made such sweet love.

When she was dressed, she walked through the house until she found him on the phone in the grand salon. His eyes lit up as they had the first time he'd seen her in the dress.

She twirled, and he nodded his approval. Then he turned away to finish his conversation.

She felt vaguely disappointed that he had not complimented her as passionately as she would have liked. Oh, what was wrong with her? Why did she feel so needy and anxious and confused when she'd had so much fun with him?

He hung up the phone. Taking her hand, he kissed it, before leading her out to the car. "I'm sorry I got angry earlier," he said when they were in the dark garage. "You've been very honest about what you want out of this relationship. I thought I was being honest, too. Apparently I didn't know what the hell I was doing."

She swallowed uneasily.

"Don't worry! No further discussion on that subject is necessary." His tone was so clipped and dismissive she felt rejected and hurt.

Later after they'd driven down a narrow, twisty road under darkening skies and through several miles of construction in tortured silence, Remy's mood seemed to improve a bit. By the time he'd parked the car, he was talking to her again. On the famous Promenade de la Croisette, he held her hand as they walked and occasionally kissed her cheek or brought her fingers to his lips as if they were an ordinary couple.

"La Croisette takes its name from a small cross that used to stand east of the bay," he said, pointing in that direction. As they walked, he pointed out other sites.

She began to relax and enjoy the promenade with its views of the Mediterranean, the Lerins Islands, and the Esterel Mountains on one side and the palms and *belle époque* hotels on the other. "If only the sun were shining, it would be perfect," she said.

"It's incredible during the film festival." He smiled. "Someday we'll come..."

Imagining it, she smiled, and then she remembered that would never happen. Still, she was glad they were past their quarrel.

A few minutes later they ran into a glamorous couple he knew. He introduced her. Not that either the man or the woman paid much attention to her. They were too busy taking turns insisting that they wanted to see more of Remy now that he'd come home for good.

The wind began to blow too briskly off the Mediterranean, so the man said a quick goodbye and would have gone, but his wife lingered. Pressing Remy's arm in a familiar fashion, she said, "Why don't we meet for drinks later?"

She didn't let go of Remy. She was beautiful in her fine linen dress and gold jewelry, and Amelia began to feel plain in comparison and wished he'd decline. Instead, he said he'd missed seeing her and suggested an hour for them to meet at Jimmy'z in the Palais de Festivals.

"And if you see any of our old crowd, invite them, as well. The more the better," he said. "I've been lonely for all of you, and I want our old crowd to meet Amelia."

Why? Did he want to be with them or just avoid being alone with her? When the dark cloud passed over them uneventfully and the sun came out, he took her shopping in several trendy boutiques. He bought Chanel for her at Bouteille's and Provençal olives for her at Cannolive. In both stores, the shop girls rushed to help him and stared at her as if fascinated.

"Did those girls know you?" she whispered when they were safely out of the second shop.

"Yes. They know my entire family."

"Why did you take me there, then?"

"A man buys expensive presents for his mistress, *n'est pas*? Maybe I'm playing your little game."

Too well, she thought, but just the same she would treasure his gifts when she was back in Oahu.

They came upon a flea market, and he laughed at her sudden enthusiasm and helped her bargain. Afterward, when she'd filled several shopping bags, he took her to the Palme d'Or on the first floor of the luxurious Hotel Martinez.

The haughty maître d' made such a fuss over Amy that he soon had her blushing. The man even lavished kisses on her hand, which seemed to please Remy immensely. Then he showed them to a wonderful corner table with a magnificent view of the promenade.

Every dish was served with a flourish. Amy ate slowly, savoring each bite. She was amazed by how many people Remy knew. Glittering couples waved at him or stopped by his table and demanded to be introduced to Amy.

Remy was charming to all, but seeing how popular he was with such a glamorous set made Amy feel his elevated place in the world. He was a *comte* and a Grand Prix champion, a celebrity in his own right. She sold old clothes and barely made enough to cover her mortgage payments.

When his friends left them alone, they sat quietly for a while, she feeling a bit strained because he felt at ease here in a dining room like this with dazzling people. Carol would fit in to this lifestyle, but Amy was much more at home in the garden of Château Serene with Etienne.

"It was a mistake to come here," he said.

Thinking he was disappointed with her, she poked at a roasted potato and rolled it around her plate.

"I'm beginning to see I don't belong with the people I've lived with all my life," he said at length. "It's as if I've lived on the surface with all of them. They know where I live, who my family is. They know I became a celebrity driving for Formula One. But they know nothing of me. You know me better than any of them."

"Me? How is that possible?"

"Think back to that day in the garden seventeen years

ago. Are you aware that no one besides me knows the truth about my birth but you and my mother? Not even my sisters."

Startled, she met his intense gaze. "I'm sorry I had to be there. I had no right to invade your privacy like that."

"It wasn't your fault. I hated you that day because I felt so humiliated. But I never should have gotten so angry with you. Now that I know you better, I'm glad you know. Maybe it's why you've become special. You know the worst. With you I have nothing to hide."

"But I felt terrible about that day for years."

His hand reached across the table and closed over hers. "I was horrible—hurt, furious, and I took it out on you." He pressed her fingers. "Our family has a great deal of false pride."

"Your family has a long history to be proud of."

"Along with dark secrets, which we keep, even from each other, so that we can remain proud and feel superior to people like you, who are more open and honest and, therefore, more fun to be with. You're so real."

"But your life and your friends are so much more exciting."

"Do you ever listen to a damn thing I say?"

"I can't imagine what your life must be like."

"I was trying to show you a little of my world this weekend. Maybe I wanted to impress you, I don't know. Maybe I wanted you to know me, the real me or the person I thought was the real me. Maybe I just wanted to show you off. I don't know why, but suddenly I'm as confused as hell."

"Show me off? That's ridiculous. I'm nobody."

"You're somebody to me."

"I run a used-clothing shop! I still live with my mother—in my own room—because housing is so expensive on Oahu, I can't afford anything better!"

"Listen to me! How is that so different from how my family lives? We've had certain properties in the family for hundreds of years. And we all stay in them as need be."

"Trust me on this," she said. "It's different. Your villa is like something out of a fairy tale. *We* park our cars on the grass in our front yard."

"Don't run yourself down to me. I'd rather be with you than any of them." He paused. "But back to that awful day we first met."

She swallowed. "I wish you'd let that go."

"When you found out who my real father was and that the *comte* hated me, I wasn't ready to face the truth and even less eager to share it. I'd worked all my life to get him to love me. You saw my pain. You understood, but when I stared into your compassionate eyes, I didn't want to accept those truths. Your sympathy forced me to face the reality, and I got angrier because all I wanted to do was run away and hide. You were very understanding. Now, you're even more so. And me, I was a jerk then and an even bigger jerk to deceive you in London. I took you to bed when you were feeling vulnerable because of your aunt's death and the breakup with your boyfriend. You were alone in a big city. And what did I do? I all but stalked you! Again, you were quick to forgive."

"Please. You're much too hard on yourself."

"Maybe. Or maybe I've been so damn anxious to prove I was more than Sando's unwanted bastard that I couldn't tolerate mistakes, especially my own. I raced, solely to prove I was something. I killed a man, a lifelong friend, and to prove what? What does any of it matter?"

"Everything matters. Or nothing matters. Take your pick. Just quit torturing yourself."

"You're so honest about who you are. Maybe it's time I started being equally honest. So what if I was born a bastard and ended up a *comte?* I loved and admired André. I didn't mean to kill him."

"It was raining. The steering jammed."

"Yes. But back then I was arrogant enough to think I could control everything—life and death. Maybe I still would be if you hadn't come to Château Serene and made your crazy bargain with me. You're making me see things in a whole new way. I've relaxed. This time with you has been special. Even here in Cannes, I've been happier than I've ever been." He lifted her hand and turned it in his. "Why is that, do you think?"

"I can't imagine. I'm sure you've been here with much more famous people and more glamorous people."

"Yes, and I was taught those were the only people who counted. I was taught to be closed-off and materialistic, to keep secrets. You have made me rethink the values of a lifetime. When I was a boy I wanted my father, or the man I believed to be my father, to notice me."

"As any little boy would."

"But he never did. When I learned Sandro Montoya was my real father I read everything I could about him. I went to all the houses where he'd lived, to the wall in Monaco where he smashed himself to pieces, searching for what? I felt nothing. It was just a wall. I went into Formula One to impress both my fathers, neither of whom had given a damn about me. During that time, I made no real friends. I was so blindly focused on winning, on proving myself to a ghost and a man who wasn't my father that I failed to connect with the people who might have cared about me."

"Stop blaming yourself."

"Famous people are just people. Being with you has taught me that what's in a person's heart matters much more than fame or status." His dark gaze was intense.

"You may think that now, but if we were serious about each other, you'd see I'm too different to fit into your world."

"Maybe it's not my world anymore. Maybe I want to be me, go to work, come home on the weekends and play soccer with my kids. All I know is that I've never enjoyed being with anyone as much as you."

"Don't," she whispered. "Don't make this more complicated than it already is. For both our sakes, you have to stay that heartless rogue I read about in the newspapers."

"Is that really who you want—the killer-womanizer in the newspapers?"

"In a week I'll be home without even a glass slipper to remember you by."

"I was beginning to hope...that you and I...that maybe you could stay a while longer. People buy old clothes even in Paris."

Terrified, she sat up stiff and straight. "Don't! Please!"

"I want to know you and for you to know me. And you want what—a few sex lessons and then to be rid of me? Is that all you want?"

She looked away. Long seconds passed. Finally, he released her hand and signaled for the bill.

She expected him to drive her home. Instead, he took her gambling at the glittering Casino Croisette where he played high-stakes games and lost enough money to make her feel tense and guilty because she was the reason for his recklessness. Then his luck turned, and he won most of it back.

"Do you always gamble so wildly?" she asked.

"Isn't that what your newspaper lover would do?"

Stung by his hard tone and words, she looked away.

He took her for drinks at Jane's Club, where they danced mechanically or sat at their little table in silence.

"I want to go home," she said.

"We're meeting people."

It was late by the time they walked into Jimmy'z. A large group of his friends sat at a large table near one of the dance floors. Céline was with them. A few minutes later, Willy Hunt, a Grand Prix driver, came over to say hi to Remy and asked if he could join them.

The music was loud and lively, and so was the conversation, which was in rapid French. It was difficult for Amy to catch much of what was said. For a while Remy was completely absorbed with his friends. But finally he turned to her, and seeing that she was watching the dancers more than she was talking, Remy pressed her fingers and asked her to dance.

Even though they were on the dance floor away from Céline, Amy couldn't relax. He moved stiffly as if he were equally tense.

"I'm sorry," she said. "Earlier you were trying to be honest, and I was the way you were that day when your father disowned you—trying to hide from my true feelings because they scare me so much. I—I know you're not the man I read about. I knew who you really were even that first night in London—because I'd read a tabloid. I think I went out with you because unconsciously I knew the papers had it all wrong. André's death hurt you just like the *comte* hurt you. I responded to that hurt, furious boy.

Only, you aren't a boy. You're a man. A very sexy man. And I'm afraid of feeling anything real for you."

"Why?"

"I think you know."

"Tell me."

"You've lived such an exciting life. You'll soon tire of someone as dull as me, so I tried to make a game of it. Sex lessons. I thought I could be like an actress playing a part. I promised you I wouldn't let myself care."

"To hell with our stupid promises!"

"Remy, I swear, the last thing I wanted to do was fall in love with you!"

"Oh, Amy, Amy. You're the best thing that has ever happened to me." He bent his head and kissed her with a wild hunger, and as she kissed him back, her heart seemed to explode with all the turbulent emotions she felt—passion, fear, desire and all sorts of insecurities. She felt more than saw the crowd at their table watching.

"Let's get the hell out of here," Remy said hoarsely. "I have to be alone with you."

"That's all I've wanted all night."

Cameras held high, two men who'd just entered the club raced toward them.

"It's him!" they yelled. *"Remy de Fournier!"*

When she turned, flashes burst in her face.

"Leave her alone, you bastards!" Furious, Remy lunged through the tables toward the two cameramen, but before he could reach them, several waiters seized the pair and hustled them back to the entrance.

"*Chérie,* we've got to get the hell out of here! The last thing I want is your name dragged into the mud because of me!"

Taking hold of her hand, he led her toward the front door, but when they stepped outside, rain was coming down in sheets. The engines of the dozen or so motorcycles that were lined up beside the building began revving. Paparazzi. Several men jumped off their bikes and swarmed Remy, shouting his name and hurling obscenities at Amy in the hope he'd look their way or try to punch them and they could then snap a valuable picture.

"Ignore them," Remy muttered, pulling her close and shielding her from the rain and cameras.

When the Alfa Romeo was being brought over, Remy's dark eyes blazed, maybe with the memory of that wet afternoon at the Circuit de Nevers at Magny-Cours. Almost defiantly, he grabbed the car keys from thc bellhop.

When she and Remy were in the car, he expertly maneuvered onto the wet street. His windshield wipers slashing violently, he called the villa and warned the guard at the gate that they might be followed.

Snapping his phone shut, he concentratcd on the heavy traffic and the motorcycles buzzing on all sides of them. From time to time a bike got too close and sloshed water all over their windows.

Despite his pale, tense face, she liked watching him drive. He exuded power and willful determination. His car was nimble, even on the slick, dark road, and he maneuvered it skillfully, changing lanes constantly to get ahead of his pursuers. Before long they were climbing toward the villa. When they reached a part of the road that was under construction, the rain started to come down even harder than before. Then the road narrowed to a single, bumpy lane walled in by concrete. Despite the narrow lane and the sheets of falling water, the motorcycles maintained their aggressive speeds. Several were ahead, two behind, and two on either side of them.

"Suicidal nuts," Remy said in clipped tones, easing off the gas pedal when brake lights flashed up ahead.

Suddenly one of the motorcyclists on the right gunned his engine and skidded just as the lane narrowed even more. To avoid being hit, Remy swerved to the left, which sent the Spider into a controlled skid straight at the concrete barricade and one of the other motorcycles.

"Damn!" Remy jerked the wheel to the right. Then slamming on the brakes because the bike on his right was too close, he veered back to the left. The Spider hit deep water and skidded wildly, whirling on two wheels before it rammed into the barricade on Remy's side. Amelia screamed as she flew forward. Then her seat belt grabbed, and everything went black.

When she regained consciousness, the windshield wipers were still on and the wind-driven rain was beating down even harder than before. She heard water hissing as if from a broken hose, and the stench of hot oil burned her nostrils.

Icy fingers pressed against her throat.

"Amelia?"

In cold horror she realized Remy was searching for her pulse. At the same time members of the paparazzi were shouting his name and jockeying to get better pictures of the famous crash victims.

A flash went off, and she blinked.

"Damn." Remy's face was inches from hers. His mouth was thin and set. Every time another flash went off, terror flicked across his white, strained face.

"Amelia!" His voice was barely more than a thread now.

"What happened?" she whispered shakily. "Did we have an accident?"

"We should be in a modern car with airbags, not this antique. Are you okay?"

"I'm fine," she said even though she'd never felt more helpless or inadequate.

"The damn fool on my right swerved straight into us. I had to cut to the left."

Funny how he remembered every detail, and she couldn't remember a thing. Still she murmured, "It wasn't your fault."

Her legs hurt. The front part of his car seemed to be crumpled in on top of them.

"Can you get me out?"

He leaned out of the car and yelled to the paparazzi to help him. When they just stood there, staring and yelling at each other, he pleaded with them, saying gasoline was everywhere and that they had to get her out just in case. Only then did they look ashamed and spring forward to assist him.

Just as Remy and two of the men lifted her from the car, she heard the first of the sirens.

The police had arrived. Remy knelt on the wet tarmac cradling her against his sodden body and shielding her blood-streaked face with his hands from the rain and the paparazzi who'd begun shooting again. Someone brought a tarp and covered them with it, but the flashes never stopped.

"Don't those damn bastards ever get enough pictures?" he muttered.

As it turned out they had way more than enough to destroy him.

Eleven

Gone was the lover who'd kissed her so passionately on the dance floor. Remy's face was as white as a death mask behind the wheel of the nondescript car he'd rented for their return to the vineyard the day following the accident. He'd barely spoken since the police chief had released him. He was free to leave Cannes, but would have to return immediately for more interviews. The police planned a thorough investigation into the accident.

"Surely they don't think you were to blame," she'd said.

Remy had cut her short. "He's just doing his job."

Despite a fierce headache and crowded, bumpy roads, Amy had devoured the morning's horrible headlines and stories about the accident. Maybe it wasn't surprising that the pounding in her head was worse than ever.

Former Grand Prix Driver Nearly Kills Mistress on Rain-Slick Road!

Police Investigation Pending!

There were pictures of Remy kissing her at Jimmy'z, and the grainy picture of Amelia that had been taken in London now had her name. Lengthy articles speculated about the exact nature of their relationship that first night in London. A waiter at the Savoy claimed they hadn't been able to keep their hands off each other. Every time Amelia reread the man's awful words, she cringed.

Worst of all the journalists compared the recent accident to the one a year ago and wondered if Remy, who'd behaved high-handedly and negligently last year, should even be allowed to have a driver's license. "Witnesses told investigators that the Alfa Romeo had been weaving in and out of traffic on the seaside promenade of Cannes earlier," she read.

Amy looked up from the newspaper to the lavender fields flying by. Was he driving too fast now? Or was she just so jittery from the accident and the terrible stories that it seemed so?

"Scared?" he muttered, easing up on the gas pedal. "Of me?"

"No. Of course not. You know the roads. You're an expert driver."

"Am I? Or am I a crazed, arrogant devil with no regard for anyone's life but my own?"

"You're just anxious to get home. And so am I."

"To be rid of me?"

"I didn't say that."

"I wouldn't blame you. I come with too much baggage—enough to sink an ocean liner."

The doctor Remy had summoned to the villa last night had ordered her to rest, but her headache and nerves had prevented her from doing more than shut her eyes.

She was shaking now, maybe partly because Remy was so upset. How she dreaded Remy's reading all the accusatory stories and seeing the awful pictures. The shots of them kissing at Jimmy'z were particularly invasive, and she hated the especially unflattering picture of Remy being held by two men as he shook his fist at a photographer last night when the man had refused to help get her out of the car.

Not that the articles about André's death weren't equally terrible. They included recent quotes from Maurice Lafitte saying Remy had always been jealous of André and had been gunning for him deliberately that day. Maurice even went so far as to accuse Remy and his mistress of trying to run him over in the village.

There were stories about Aunt Tate and the *comte* and the Matisse he'd given her. Anonymous village sources recounted in lurid detail Aunt Tate's love affair and marriage with the late *comte*. They said that the young *comte*'s affair with Tate's niece didn't surprise them, that the niece was an American gold-digger just like her aunt, that the niece was refusing to sell the world-famous Matisse back to the French family to whom it had rightfully belonged for a century, that she planned to leave the country with it.

Without looking at Remy again, Amy folded the last newspaper and laid it in her lap on top of the others.

Remy came to a crossroads, touched a blinker and then turned onto a back road, which was fringed on both sides with lavender. She knew from her walks that the rural lane cut a swath through the vineyards that led straight to Château Serene.

"If you don't go back to Hawaii quickly, there'll be even

worse stories," he said. "Now that they've tasted fresh blood, yours, they won't let up. In all probability they'll be waiting to pounce on you at Château Serene."

"Surely not."

"Whatever you do, don't grant an interview. They'll twist your words to prove their viewpoint."

When they rounded the last curve, she gasped when she saw a television truck, three motorcycles and two men with binoculars and cameras standing at the ready by the gate.

"Oh, no," she murmured as the men rushed toward their car, cameras held high.

"So now you know what it is like to be Remy de Fournier's mistress. You will be hounded like this until you leave France. Not a fate I would wish on anyone. If we continue to see each other, they will want pictures of our every assignation. We may even find a photographer under your aunt's bed."

"That's disgusting."

"You heard the police chief. I have to be back in Cannes tomorrow."

"I'll go with you if that would help."

"No! You should cut your losses."

"But—"

"Don't you understand we've lost our chance?"

"Is there no standing up to them? Are you going to let them ruin your life forever?"

"Look, I learned a long time ago that I'm not in control of what is written about me. I'm trying to protect you. You have to go home as soon as possible."

"But I love you!"

"If you decide to sign the sales contract early, I'll do

everything in my power to expedite the purchase so you can leave without any extra hassles. But I must warn you—buying and selling real estate is not as simple in France as it is in the U.S. We have many bureaucrats in need of salaries. There will be many documents and much red tape. And finding a home for the Matisse won't be easy, but I do know a reputable art dealer who could help you."

"Bottom line—you want me gone."

"It's for the best."

"So, it's over."

He didn't deny it.

Her chest felt strange and tight. Her eyes burned, but she could think of nothing to say. He wanted her gone. It didn't matter that she'd told him she loved him.

Fifty yards later, he turned into the drive that led up to the château.

Without a word, he braked, got out and carried her bags to the door. She let herself out of the car more slowly and walked gingerly toward the house. When she reached him, he didn't smile. He didn't touch her or kiss her or even offer to carry her bags inside as he would have in the past. All seemed so frozen and changed between them. It was as if the past few hours had killed every tender feeling he'd ever had for her.

"Do you want to come in?" she asked.

He shook his head. "Don't you get it? Photographers with high-powered lenses could be hiding anywhere to take our pictures," he muttered.

"No more making love out by your pool, either." He opened the door and slid her bags inside. "No telling what technologies these guys have. They're like spies. They can probably take pictures in the dark."

"Is this goodbye, then?" she whispered.

"Like I said—tomorrow I have to talk to the police chief. I don't know what will be involved or how long I'll be gone. Or if I can satisfy him."

"You should let me come."

"If we don't see each other, the reporters will leave in a few days, and you'll have your privacy back."

"What about you?"

"You forget, I'm an old hand at being lynched by the press. I'll survive." He stared unseeingly in front of him.

Would he? Was he already a haunted man on the run from his demons again?

"Be sure to call me. At least tell me how the investigation goes."

He shook his head. "I don't think that's smart. There are lots of techies out there who know how to listen in on cell-phone conversations."

"Then this is really goodbye?"

"It's for your own good," he muttered. "I knew better than to let you become involved with me."

She bit her lip and looked anywhere but at him. Then her head began to pound even more viciously.

"Remy, please…please don't be like this."

"Goodbye," he said in a soft, tender voice. "I won't ever forget you. And I will call…in a few weeks, when you're safely home and the bastards are chasing new prey. Hopefully I'll be able to tell you that all this has blown over."

"But on the dance floor at Jimmy'z, we said… I—I thought that you and I—"

"Dammit, I drove you into that wall! I was driving an old car! The seat belt didn't work. I nearly killed you! Now these jackals are writing awful stories about you! Who the hell knows what the police will accuse me of next? What does it take to show you it has to be over?"

When her telephone began to ring, he began backing away. "You'd better answer that. It's probably your mother or one of your friends wanting to grill you, chastise you for having anything to do with a man like me."

"Remy, no! Don't leave me like this!"

"I have to do what's right, for a change. We always knew this had to end. I'm sorry I let things go so far."

She stared at his face and felt nothing. He was leaving her forever, and she felt nothing. How was that possible? Shock?

He took a deep breath and stared at her for a long moment. Then he turned and walked back down the drive to his car. He got in, slammed the door and drove away, as always without looking back.

The phone had stopped ringing by the time she went inside, but within five minutes it began again.

Thinking it was her mother and she might as well get the interrogation over with, she picked it up.

"Baby! It's Fletcher! Hey, you sound like you're just next door."

Fletcher, who never called, wanted to know how she was and what she was up to. Last of all, he said he was sorry about the girls and for how he'd acted, that he'd been awful, and that he wanted her back.

"I got a real job—selling insurance—to prove to you that I'm ready to grow up, baby."

"Don't do anything rash on my account, Fletcher."

"Is this cold attitude because of that count? There's no way a rich guy like him would be interested in you for anything except that painting or the vineyard."

"You don't know anything about him."

"You're too—"

Much to his surprise, she hung up on him.

Her headache, if possible, was worse, and her eyes burned. Feeling lost, she walked through the house, her footsteps echoing hollowly. She stared at the stacks of boxes and at her aunt's things that still needed to be packed. She felt overwhelmed as she wondered how many more hours it would take before she had everything packed.

The job seemed endless, and someday she would have to figure out what to do about the Matisse, too.

Instead of unpacking her suitcases or lying down, she fixed herself a cup of tea, went outside and stared at the blue chaise longues by the pool until a slight movement from the trees warned her that someone was probably spying on her and taking pictures.

Running back inside, she slammed and locked the door. Then she shut all the windows and drew the curtains.

Alone in the house, the long, lonely day stretched ahead of her. Would her head ever stop pounding?

She was almost grateful that she had no mind, no heart, no senses. Still, she knew that when they came back she'd be in hell.

What would she do without Remy?

Why was it so wrong to love him?

On the second day after Remy had dropped her off, when she'd heard nothing from him, she was beside herself with grief and worry. She wished Remy would call and tell her how the investigation was going. Was he in even more trouble? She grew frantic from missing him.

Thus far, her only source was the media. All the newspapers ran editorials demanding that the police take a firm stand with him. The talking heads on television wanted the same thing. To buy newspapers, she had to drive into the village or send Etienne, and this meant dealing with the reporters camped at her gates. They followed her, yelling at her and demanding interviews.

Why couldn't she forget how much she'd enjoyed Remy in bed and out of it? Constantly she told herself Remy was right not to want to see her. What future could they possibly have? She might as well suffer the pains of withdrawal now.

To stay busy she'd contacted his estate agent and told him she was ready to sell the vineyard. He brought the documents over, and they discussed them. In between packing more boxes, she even signed a few.

She was tired by the time the sun began to go down, lingering forever on the horizon. Never had a day seemed longer or more unbearable. She was thinking maybe a shower would make her feel better when the phone rang.

Remy? She dived for it, answering in eager, breathless French.

"Et ma fille, Mademoiselle Amelia Weatherbee, *avec château?"* said an all-too-familiar voice with a terrible American accent.

"Mother, this is me!" Wisely Amy refrained from correcting her mother's French.

"Why haven't you called?"

"I was going to!"

"Are you his mistress or aren't you?"

"Puh-leeze! That's such an out-of-date term, Mom!" Not that she hadn't used it herself, but that was different.

"From what the papers say and from what Tate used to tell me, your race-car driver is a fast sort and much worse than Fletcher. Enough said. And by the way, Fletcher's actually called. You may be hearing from him."

"I can't believe you discussed this with Fletcher."

"I didn't have to discuss anything. One of his more literate friends saw the stories on the Internet."

"Well, he called. He wants me back."

"You broke up with him?"

"Before I came here."

"Well, I hope you said hell no."

"My decision. Not yours."

"Which gives me chills! So how can you fall for a man even worse than Fletcher?"

"I'm a grown woman, Mother, so stop with all the questions and assumptions!"

"Then act like one. The de Fourniers despised your aunt Tate, and she never got her name dragged through the mud. I can't imagine what they must think of you. Carol certainly never embarrassed me or herself like this."

Amy took a deep breath and counted to ten—twice.

"When are you coming home?"

"Soon. I do have a few papers to sign and a little more packing."

"Carol is most concerned. She'd really like you to stop by in London. If you don't, who knows when you girls will see each other again? Besides, you could use some sound advice from a rational individual like your brilliant sister. At least she's made something of her life. She's a barrister, and she's married to—"

"Must you always throw Carol at me?"

"Just trying to be helpful, dear."

"Well, then, if that's the truth, it would be really, really helpful if you could watch the shop a bit longer."

"Of course, dear. I've been having the time of my life running your shop. Not that I don't have a legal pad full of helpful suggestions for you. The way you order…"

"Okay. Okay. Then if you'll really watch the shop, I would love to stop in London, although I'm not really in the mood for advice from my brilliant sister."

"You never are, dear."

Amy hung up, furious, but at least her anger toward her mother distracted her from worrying so much about Remy.

"I can't believe it! 'Probably something I ate, or jet lag,' you said. My, what a cool liar you were! And I bought it! Me! Brilliant, little ol' me, big-shot lady barrister who can see through liars like they're made of glass. And now you say you have a headache. Ha!"

"Did Mother put you up to this?"

"As if I needed to be told to call my *notorious* sister when all my friends are just dying to know what's going on." Carol giggled. "They're all simply wild to meet you, too. If you come, Steve and I'll throw a big party to show you off. You're a celebrity!"

"*No party!* And I don't need this! Not right now!"

"None of us blame you one bit. Your *comte* sounds positively dishy. Rich, too! And a celebrity! If he's half as good in bed as he looks, I may fight you for him!"

"Carol!"

"Just kidding. But I do want details."

"Carol, I'm sorry I lied to you, but I really *do* have a headache tonight."

"Right."

"For your information I've had one ever since the accident. So I'm going to hang up, stare at the ceiling and sulk if you don't stop with the teasing. This is not a funny situation."

"Oh, my God, you're not in love with him, are you? Amy? You're *not*, are you? Because he's a *comte*...and he's had all those women! He couldn't possibly care about—"

"Carol, please, I'm begging you—back down."

"Okay, okay. I'll save it until you get here. But I want to hear all about him then. If you've been sleeping with him, you've got to tell me *everything* because, and I hate to say this, a good marriage can become so dull, so routine after a few years. Not that the sex isn't kinda nice."

A phone call from her mother and another one from her sister in one night! Amy was shaking when Carol finally hung up.

She walked into the kitchen and poured herself a tall glass of chablis. As she sipped it, the wine both soothed and made her more vulnerable to her feelings.

She missed Remy. For weeks she'd seen him every day. What if he was in serious trouble with the police? What if there was something she could say to them that would help him? She had to talk to him.

Since he'd warned her against using cell phones, she called the Château de Fournier instead. But as the phone rang, Amy felt panic rising within her. When a woman answered, she almost slammed the phone down.

"Is...is Remy there?"

"Just a moment please."

She bit her lip. Then another woman came on the line. "This is Céline."

"I—I want Remy."

"I'm sorry. He went to Cannes yesterday."

"I know. This is Amy Weatherbee. Do you have any idea how the investigation is going?"

"I know who you are, Mademoiselle Weatherbee. We thought he'd be back today. But he hasn't even called."

"Well, if you hear from him, would you tell him to call me, please?"

"Of course, mademoiselle. Excuse me…"

When Amy heard muffled voices, she had the feeling that Céline had covered the phone to speak to someone else.

Céline returned almost at once. "I'm sorry about the interruption. The *comtesse* would like to speak to you."

The *comtesse*'s voice was cold. "Madamemoiselle Weatherbee, I'm delighted about the sale. Does this mean you will be leaving soon?"

"As soon as possible."

"I don't wonder, all these awful reporters snooping about. Céline can't even wander down to the village without having one of the beasts pop out and take her picture."

"I'm sorry about all that," Amy said even as she wondered what Céline was doing in the village if Remy wasn't coming back.

"I did warn Remy. He should have protected you," his mother said.

Amy saw no reason to tell her he'd tried. "If he calls, would you please tell him I'd like to see him before I go."

"I don't think that will be possible. His secretary and a good friend of his are getting married in Paris. He's going to be best man. It's rather sudden. As soon as Remy's finished in Cannes, he has a direct flight to Paris."

"So, he…he has no plans to return to Château de Fournier?"

"Not as far as I know." The *comtesse*'s quiet voice held icy triumph.

Amy's eyes felt hot as she hung up, but she didn't cry.

Like Cinderella after the ball, her world was reduced to cinders.

It was over. In a few days she'd be home.

Twelve

The cicadas were roaring as Amy sat dully beside the pool and sipped black, double-strength coffee that was so hot it burned her tongue. Between sips, she bit into her buttery breakfast croissant. Make that her second croissant, both of which had been slathered thickly with orange marmalade.

She was full, but still eating. She shouldn't take another bite, but she'd been on something of an eating binge since she'd talked to the *comtesse* two days ago. Not that she wanted to think about how tight her jeans were. She simply wanted to eat and forget.

Funny how everything about Château Serene made her miss Remy. The sweet scent of lavender made her remember making love to him out here under the stars. The glimmering water made her think of the times they'd skinny-dipped. Under those pine trees, he'd held her and they'd made their bargain.

Such thoughts were an indulgence. She had to quit torturing herself. With a supreme effort of will, she looked past the pool to the lavender that rolled toward the distant mountains. The château and vineyard were a picture postcard come to life. Her heart ached at the thought of leaving it all forever.

She loved him. She knew that no matter how long she lived or who else she loved or what children she might have, she would never forget this poignantly lovely place, and it would always remind her of him.

How strange. Remy had taught her to be sexy, but it didn't matter because she wanted no one but him. He hadn't just imparted skills. He'd given himself. He was the magic that made her come alive in bed.

Suddenly, above the humming of the cicadas, she heard a car sweep up the drive. Her stomach tightened in both anticipation and dread.

Even though she knew Remy was supposed to be in Paris, she got up and ran around to the front of the château, anyway. And oh, how painfully her stomach knotted at the sight of the tall, slim blonde in pristine, white slacks, her hair an elegant coil at the nape of her slender neck.

Céline, too lovely for words as usual, was knocking on the front door. Amelia felt like running away and hiding. Instead, she called, "Hi, there."

Tension flowing out of every invisible pore of her creamy face, Céline jerked around. Her eyes were as huge and desolate as Amy's heart. "Oh, there you are," she said without the least bit of enthusiasm.

Why wasn't Céline in Paris? Amy wondered. She said, "I—I was just having breakfast in the garden."

"I thought maybe you'd already left for America. I promise I won't keep you long."

"Would you like some coffee?"

Céline shook her head and then changed her mind when she saw Amy's cup. After Amy prepared the coffee to Céline's liking and they'd talked about all the boxes in every room and the dates the movers would come for them and which was the best moving company in the area, Amelia led her out to the garden.

"I could tell you were probably expecting Remy when you heard the car," Céline said softly. "You looked unhappy to see me."

"But he's in Paris."

"Yes. I do dislike disappointing you, but I *had* to see you." As if at a loss for words, she stared at Amy. "I—I have only one question." A desperate look chased across her pretty face. "Do you love him?"

Amy jerked her chin higher.

Céline's blue eyes were luminous, and she was twisting her hands. "I *have* to know because…because you see, I love him. I love him very much. I've loved him all my life."

Each word felt like a blade cutting Amy's heart. How stylish and beautiful Céline was with her flawless skin and doll-like features. She was much lovelier than Carol. Remy and she would make a beautiful couple. What darling children they would have—dark-headed boys and blond girls. Little weekend soccer players. Amy winced.

"If you don't love him, Mademoiselle Weatherbee, let him go. Because like I said, I do love him. So very much."

"Shouldn't you be telling these things to him? After all, I'm going home—alone. If he's in Paris and you live there, why are you here?"

"I don't believe he's ready to love anyone right now. He isn't over what happened last year. But in time, he will be."

"And you'll be there?"

"If he wants me to be."

"And does he?"

"We dated when we were young. But something happened to him. I never knew what, and he grew so remote. A year or so later, he went into Formula One. He drove himself with a vengeance, and I never knew why. None of us did. He was so different, so competitive and so ruthlessly ambitious on and off the track. He was not the same sweet, gentle boy I'd loved. But even during those years I would see him from time to time because his sisters were such dear friends of mine."

"His sisters?"

"They encouraged me not to give up on him. Racing careers are often brutal and short. We thought that if he survived, he might become his old self again and we would marry. So, I waited. But he won more and more races. He grew famous. Women threw themselves at him, and I saw him so little that I gave up and married another man. And I was happy. But not like I'd been happy with Remy. Still, my husband, Ivan, was good to me, and I was content. Then Ivan's plane crashed in the Alps the same month Remy had his awful accident."

"I'm so sorry."

"Yes. It was terrible. I was numb for months. But something terrible like that teaches you, too. I can understand what Remy is going through. I knew André when he was a boy, you see. I understand suffering and what it is to be damaged, to blame yourself. I had encouraged my husband to fly that day. I believe that I can love Remy and understand him and help him get over André as no one else can. His family adores me. Especially his mother. Family approval is so important when it comes to marriage, don't you agree? And you would never have that, would you?"

Amy was cold and shivering in the heat long before Céline finished. Whatever hope she'd had of Remy changing his mind in a few months and coming to find her vanished like smoke blown away by the wind. Céline would not let that happen.

Amy must have said goodbye as she walked Céline around to her car, but later she had no memory of even leaving the garden.

As she stared at the lavender and pines, she knew that everything Céline had said made perfect sense. Céline would make Remy a perfect wife. Once Amy was gone, he would forget their brief time and turn to Céline.

The only role Amy would ever play was the one she had chosen—to be his mistress for a month.

Their month was over.

Thirteen

Standing beside Pierre-Louis at the city hall in the Fourth Arrondisement, Remy ground the wedding rings into his palm even as he forced himself to relax.

He was here. He'd actually made it on time to the wedding. He'd been exonerated—again. More than exonerated. The chief had blamed the paparazzi.

The Cannes police chief had grilled him relentlessly for hours before finally releasing him a mere forty-five minutes before his plane for Paris had been due to depart.

Much relieved, Remy knew the police chief's decision would anger the bloodthirsty media. No doubt, every journalist in France would be howling for his head.

He wanted to call Amy and tell her he was a free man, but she was the one person he could never share his thoughts or feelings with again. With much effort he concentrated on the enraptured faces of Marie-Elise and

Pierre-Louis. Only slowly did their happiness make his own tension and dark mood lighten.

The wedding ceremony was as romantic as the city hall was dull and official-looking, with its blue-and-white-trimmed walls, French flag and severe portrait of the French president. But if ever there was proof of the power of love to transform two people, the couple's shining eyes as they looked at each other were the living evidence of it. Gone was Remy's plain, efficient secretary hiding fearfully behind her thick glasses and her ill-fitting clothes. Today she was a blushing vision of utter femininity in her ivory-lace gown and clouds of tulle. The froth became the bride. Pierre-Louis was tanned, muscular and robust, even fitter than he'd been before the accident and his tragic divorce.

One minute Remy was staring at Marie-Elise's glowing face, and the next he was losing himself in the memory of a pair of fine, hazel eyes that had been equally radiant when they'd devoured his on the dance floor at Jimmy'z. Her lips had been so soft when he'd kissed her after she'd told him she loved him. She'd put her heart and soul in that kiss and offered herself to him forever.

Love. It had the power to give fresh hope, new meaning and immense happiness to anyone who dared to risk his or her soul again.

Why the hell was he letting her go?

For her own good, you fool. You don't deserve her.

But if she loves you…

As he focused on the bride and groom, he couldn't help visualizing Amy in a white dress and veil.

Slowly the dull, hopeless self-loathing that had afflicted him ever since André's death lifted. He had to call Amy.

No sooner had he made this decision than he began to

chafe for the ceremony to be over and for the wedding documents to be signed, because now, at last, he knew what he had to do.

He had to find Amy and see if she would still have him.

But when the ceremony was over, Pierre-Louis reminded him he'd promised to stay for the reception. As the best man he could not refuse.

Then at the reception, Taylor and several members of his Formula One team showed up, including his two top drivers, and, wouldn't you know it, they all joined forces with Pierre-Louis.

"You planned this, didn't you, Pierre-Louis?" Remy accused when he was surrounded.

"You did say if I ever wanted anything, you'd be there. I want you to listen to what Taylor has to say."

Cornering him, the men pressed him to reconsider joining their team.

Taylor, a tall forceful man with a shock of thick, gray hair, said, "We want you because you weren't just a brilliant driver, you were intuitive. You found speed that was beyond your intellectual limit and then you notched it even higher, so much higher than anyone else's. You were incredible. You know the business on a profound level, as well. A man with your talents could do so much for Formula One."

As Remy stood shaking his head beside Pierre-Louis and the other men while they showered him with praise and told him about their new car and invited him to help with its testing, as they described in detail what he could do for them, he began to feel a flicker of the old excitement and heady self-confidence that had driven him for so long and had made him one hell of a competitive Formula One driver. His head stopped shaking. Formula One had been his life for a lot of years. Maybe this was his second chance to make things right.

Did grief have a life of its own and a death, as well? Suddenly more than anything he wanted Amy. If he felt alive enough to listen to Taylor again, it was solely because of her.

The mistral tore over the mountains and ripped through the pines as Remy stood in the garden staring at the pool and blue chaise longue where they'd made love. A shutter banged. The house was empty of Tate's things. All the boxes had been moved.

Amy was gone.

What had he expected? He had told her it was over, and he'd sent her away.

With slumped shoulders, he walked around the crumbling stone house where Céline waited in the car. He didn't feel like being with her, but she'd insisted on coming.

Even though Amy's leaving without even writing him a note or saying goodbye was his fault, he felt as small and lost as he had the day he'd learned the *comte* hated him because he was Sando Montoya's bastard.

Remy got in the car and jammed his key in the ignition. But instead of starting the car, he just sat there.

"Why don't you start the car?" Céline whispered.

"We've got to end this thing."

"What are you talking about?"

"This. Us. Whatever the hell you're doing. Your surprise visits. Your sudden coziness with my mother."

"But I thought—"

"I thought I made myself clear."

"But you said in a month…"

"It hasn't been a month. Not that that matters."

"But she's gone."

"I'm sorry, Céline."

"I thought that when she left, maybe you and I…"

"I'm sorry."

"But if she's not coming back…"

"Don't say that. Don't even think it. I've got to find her and make her understand that I was wrong, so wrong about everything."

"You love her?"

"I've never been in love before, so I've behaved rather stupidly. But, yes, I guess I am in love."

"Oh, Remy, then I've done something truly terrible, so terrible I don't know if you can ever forgive me."

He looked at her. "I've done terrible things and have needed forgiveness and compassion myself. Why don't you try me?"

"It's about Amy…."

Geography. Songs. Scents. These are the things that transport you in time and bring old memories so acutely into focus that they hurt again. Thus, London, with its black cabs and double-decker red buses and cool, humid air made Amy long too keenly for Remy as she walked toward Carol's flat after a long day of shopping.

The straps of her heavy shopping bags cut into her arms. Her feet ached, but she stopped at the exact spot where Remy had bumped into her and knocked her bags to the ground.

For a long moment she held her breath. Everything was the same, but nothing was. Loss filled her. How long would it take before she wasn't haunted every minute of every hour by his absence? If only she could make a wish and turn the clock back and have him here.

She bit her lips. Visiting Carol had seemed like such a good idea, just the thing to help her get over Remy, just as shopping today at Camden Market had seemed like a good idea after her mother had faxed a list of things for her to shop for. But she'd thought of Remy all day, and there had been no fun in any of her purchases.

Carol was coming into the city to take her to dinner, and she needed to get ready. But she dreaded Carol's questioning and advice. Glancing at her watch, Amy realized she'd better hurry. Perfect Carol was always on time.

Just as she was about to resume walking, a tall, dark man with lithe, long-legged strides dashed across the street straight toward her.

When she turned, he slowed his pace. Even before she really looked at him, her skin began to prickle with excitement. Her breathing became very fast and shallow, and her legs suddenly felt like spaghetti.

A lock of black hair fell over his brow and he pushed it back, and the gesture was so familiar her breath caught.

"Have you been out buying see-through knickers again?"

"Remy? *Remy!*"

Then her bags were falling from her hands, their contents spilling everywhere. But she was running and yelling his name over and over again, too happy to care.

"I love you," he said as he folded her into his arms. "I love you. I hope I'm not too late."

"All that matters is that you're here now."

"And I'll be here forever if you'll have me. I need a wife, not a mistress. Will you marry me?"

All the love in her heart flew to him. She wanted to say yes, yes, yes, but she was so filled with emotion, the words caught in her throat, so she kissed him, instead, long and steadily. Forever.

She was going to be his *comtesse*. That would take some getting used to for a lot of people, like his mother and his sisters. And maybe her own mother, too.

Or maybe it wouldn't.

"My mother always told me that fairy tales were real. She used to promise me that someday I'd grow up and be a princess."

"I'm afraid you'll only be a *comtesse*."

"Being your *comtesse* is way better than being an ordinary princess," she said. "Will we live in your château?"

"Not unless you want to live with my mother. I have an apartment in Paris. My office is there."

"Definitely Paris."

"When you give birth to our first soccer player, we'll have to look for a bigger place."

"Oh, Remy, I'm so happy."

"Me, too."

He kissed her again, and he didn't stop for a very long time.

* * * * *

THOROUGHBRED LEGACY

The stakes are high when it comes to love,
horse racing, family secrets
and broken promises.

A new exciting Harlequin continuity
series coming soon!
Led by New York Times *bestselling author*
Elizabeth Bevarly
FLIRTING WITH TROUBLE

Here's a preview!

THE DOOR CLOSED behind them, throwing them into darkness and leaving them utterly alone. And the next thing Daniel knew, he heard himself saying, "Marnie, I'm sorry about the way things turned out in Del Mar."

She said nothing at first, only strode across the room and stared out the window beside him. Although he couldn't see her well in the darkness—he still hadn't switched on a light...but then, neither had she—he imagined her expression was a little preoccupied, a little anxious, a little confused.

Finally, very softly, she said, "Are you?"

He nodded, then, worried she wouldn't be able to see the gesture, added, "Yeah. I am. I should have said goodbye to you."

"Yes, you should have."

Actually, he thought, there were a lot of things he should have done in Del Mar. He'd had *a lot* riding on the Pacific Classic, and even more on his entry, Little Joe, but after meeting Marnie, the Pacific Classic had been the last thing on Daniel's mind. His loss at Del Mar had pretty much ended his career before it had even begun, and he'd had to start all over again, rebuilding from nothing.

He simply had not then and did not now have room in his life for a woman as potent as Marnie Roberts. He was a horseman first and foremost. From the time he was a schoolboy, he'd known what he wanted to do with his life—be the best possible trainer he could be.

He had to make sure Marnie understood—and he understood, too—why things had ended the way they had eight years ago. He just wished he could find the words to do that. Hell, he wished he could find the *thoughts* to do that.

"You made me forget things, Marnie, things that I really needed to remember. And that scared the hell out of me. Little Joe should have won the Classic. He was by far the best horse entered in that race. But I didn't give him the attention he needed and deserved that week, because all I could think about was you. Hell, when I woke up that morning all I wanted to do was lie there and look at you, and then wake you up and make love to you again. If I hadn't left when I did—the way I did—I might still be lying there in that bed with you, thinking about nothing else."

"And would that be so terrible?" she asked.

"Of course not," he told her. "But that wasn't why I was

in Del Mar," he repeated. "I was in Del Mar to win a race. That was my job. And my work was the most important thing to me."

She said nothing for a moment, only studied his face in the darkness as if looking for the answer to a very important question. Finally she asked, "And what's the most important thing to you now, Daniel?"

Wasn't the answer to that obvious? "My work," he answered automatically.

She nodded slowly. "Of course," she said softly. "That is, after all, what you do best."

Her comment, too, puzzled him. She made it sound as if being good at what he did was a bad thing.

She bit her lip thoughtfully, her eyes fixed on his, glimmering in the scant moonlight that was filtering through the window. And damned if Daniel didn't find himself wanting to pull her into his arms and kiss her. But as much as it might have felt as if no time had passed since Del Mar, there were eight years between now and then. And eight years was a long time in the best of circumstances. For Daniel and Marnie, it was virtually a lifetime.

So Daniel turned and started for the door, then halted. He couldn't just walk away and leave things as they were, unsettled. He'd done that eight years ago and regretted it.

"It *was* good to see you again, Marnie," he said softly. And since he was being honest, he added, "I hope we see each other again."

She didn't say anything in response, only stood silhouetted against the window with her arms wrapped around her in a way that made him wonder whether she was doing it because she was cold, or if she just needed something—someone—to hold on to. In either case, Daniel understood. There was an emptiness clinging to him that he suspected would be there for a long time.

* * * * *

THOROUGHBRED LEGACY

coming soon wherever books are sold!

COMING NEXT MONTH

#1873 JEALOUSY & A JEWELLED PROPOSITION—Yvonne Lindsay
Diamonds Down Under
Determined to avenge his family's name, this billionaire sets out to take over his biggest competition...and realizes his ex may be the perfect weapon for revenge.

#1874 COLE'S RED-HOT PURSUIT—Brenda Jackson
After a night of passion, a wealthy sheriff will stop at nothing to get the woman back into his bed. And he always gets what he wants.

#1875 SEDUCED BY THE ENEMY—Sara Orwig
Platinum Grooms
He has a score to settle with his biggest business rival. Seducing his enemy's daughter proves to be the perfect way to have his revenge.

#1876 THE KING'S CONVENIENT BRIDE—Michelle Celmer
Royal Seductions
An arranged marriage turns all too real when the king falls for his convenient wife. Don't miss the second book in the series, also available this June!

#1877 THE ILLEGITIMATE PRINCE'S BABY—Michelle Celmer
Royal Seductions
The playboy prince proposes a mock engagement...until his pretend fiancée becomes pregnant! Don't miss the first book in this series, also on sale this June!

#1878 RICH MAN'S FAKE FIANCÉE—Catherine Mann
The Landis Brothers
Caught in a web of tabloid lies, their only recourse is a fake engagement. But the passion they feel for one another is all too real.

SDCNM0508